THE BLOOD OF ENGLISHMEN

An Anthology

History Through Fiction

The Blood of Englishmen © copyright 2026 History Through Fiction. All rights reserved. No part of this book may be reproduced in any form whatsoever, by photography or xerography or by any other means, by broadcast or transmission, by translation into any kind of language, nor by recording electronically or otherwise, without permission in writing from the author, except by a reviewer, who may quote brief passages in critical articles or reviews.

NO AI TRAINING: Without in any way limiting the author's exclusive rights under copyright, any use of this publication to "train" generative artificial intelligence (AI) technologies to generate text is expressly prohibited. All rights to license uses of this work for generative AI training and development of machine learning language models are reserved.

ISBNs: 978-1-963452-40-2 (pb);
978-1-963452-41-9 (eBook)

Book Cover Design: Steph Ross
Interior Book Design: Inanna Arthen, inannaarthen.com

Library of Congress Control Number: 2026934474

First Printing: 2026
Printed in the United States of America

Contents

San Francisco is Buckled, San Francisco is Burning
    Rachel Henderson 4
Lucky
    Zena Ryder 14
Body #311
    Christopher DeWitt 21
The Violinist
    Ezra Harker Shaw 36
The Blood of Englishmen
    Cecil Beckett 52
No Shelter
    Nicole M. Babb 61
The Presbyterian Settee
    Rob Hardy 71
The God of Sight
    Morgan Want 82
The Bright Leaf Legacy
    Jacqueline Van Hoewyk 95
Diary of an Empire
    Shay Galloway 110
Acknowledgments 119
About History Through Fiction 121

San Francisco is Buckled, San Francisco is Burning

Rachel Henderson

SAN FRANCISCO IS BURNING, and that's a real shame—but Mr. Thomas Hardesty's pocket watch is still missing.

Eighteen-karat yellow gold, sapphire inlay, valued at over $10,000. Stolen two days before the earthquake by a girl who called herself Bettie. Hardesty met her at the Poodle Dog, where they nibbled on Toke Point oysters, pickled walnuts and caviar. She had a port-wine stain on her forehead and a missing pinkie finger on her left hand. He didn't mind—company is company—and there was an agreeable mischief about her, the way she played with his mustache, ran her hands across his chest, stroked his knee beneath the table. Bold as brass. Must've lifted the watch from his inside pocket before he left, boiled-owl drunk, around midnight—alone, of course, because girls with port-wine stains are fine for the Poodle Dog, but you don't bring them back to the Palace Hotel. It was morning before he noticed it was gone.

"Already in last week's report, Mr. Hardesty," Detective Yount says. "Everything. To the letter."

"Is it really?"

"We're very thorough."

"Well, I had to make sure. Considering my watch is still missing."

Yount blinks. His eyes sting—how could they not, after five days of smoke rolling through the streets, slithering under doorways, throttling a city on its deathbed—and he resists the urge to rub them.

Hardesty leans forward in his chair. His eyes are clear.

"As I told your chief, Detective, I would appreciate a bit more urgency on this matter."

"Urgency!"

"Yes, Detective, urgency. A small tip of the hat by your department, an acknowledgment I've been waylaid—miserably waylaid. I should've been halfway to Boston by now. Do you realize what day it is?"

Yount silently counts forward from last Wednesday—stumbles on the number—starts over.

"Sunday," Hardesty says. "I'm over forty-eight hours waylaid, because my watch is still missing. It's still missing because you, Detective, have not done your job. I said as much to your chief in my telegram this morning, and his response was sympathetic. Extremely sympathetic."

Yount closes his notebook and slips it inside his jacket.

"Understand?" Hardesty asks.

"I do."

Hardesty's mustache twitches. He leans back, brushes a nugget of ash from his pant leg.

"I was sorry to leave the Palace. This hotel is shabby. Bad breakfasts, terrible beds—like sleeping on a pile of rocks. Can't be helped, I know—but for heaven's sake. Not so much as a goose down pillow?"

Today is Sunday, and San Francisco is still burning.

Yount stares at the building that used to be the Poodle Dog. Scorched bricks and broken glass litter the sidewalk. He picks up a scrap of crispy paper—Chateaubriand, 1.50, Chicken Jerusalem, 2.00. His stomach groans. There was free bread at the station earlier this morning, but he only ate a few mouthfuls—it was sandy-dry, tasted like spoiled milk. Worlds apart from his sister Ellen's bread. Or her butter-crumb biscuits. Or her cinnamon-spiced rolls.

His stomach groans again.

Chicken Jerusalem.

He wonders what it is, and if Ellen ever heard of it. Their Mission apartment was always thick with kitchen smells, but familiar ones, phantoms of their late mother's cookery: onions, eggs, pork, garlic. Nothing fancy—nothing French. No pickled walnuts or caviar for the Yount family.

It feels wrong, being out and about in the city without a bellyful of Ellen's cooking. Sacrilegious.

But like Hardesty said, can't be helped.

"Hey, fella! You shouldn't be here!"

Yount looks up. Two soldiers are hustling up the street toward him, Army-issued frowns on their soot-smeared faces. One is cradling a whiskey jug.

"I'm with the police," Yount says.

"The hell you say."

Yount digs out his badge—it's the temporary sort, just a piece of cardboard with the chief's signature, issued to the men who lost their credentials in the quake. The soldier with the jug squints at it, and his frown deepens.

"Police shouldn't be here neither. We're on orders to keep all citizens away."

"And shoot looters," his companion slurs. There's a penny-sized gash on his chin. The blood looks fresh.

"I'm not a looter."

"Could be you are, could be you aren't. How're we supposed to tell?"

"Listen, fella," the soldier with the jug says, "we need you to get out of here. If you're looking for a place to stay, head over to the Presidio."

"I'm not looking for shelter. I'm looking for a woman. Young, port-wine stain on her forehead, missing pinkie on her left hand. Goes by Bettie."

"Sweetheart of yours?"

"Suspected thief. Gentleman claims she stole his pocket watch last week."

The soldiers' mouths slip open—their laughter begins in unison. A barrage of liquor-soaked snorts and giggles pummel Yount in the face. He takes a step back, but has to admit it's a welcome change, getting a whiff of something besides smoke.

"You keep looking for that criminal, mister policeman," the bloody soldier says. "I just know you're gonna find her. Sure, you got justice on your side!"

"Check the Presidio!"

"Yeah, the Presidio. All the evil ladies are having themselves a rendezvous at the Presidio."

"Go to the Presidio!"

Yount hurries up the street, the soldiers' jeers biting his heels. Smoke fills his lungs with each step. He races past ruined buildings until he finds more people, soldiers and civilians alike, shuffling along the sidewalks and huddling in the alleyways; he peers at their faces, all too ash-coated to show a port wine stain, all too miserable to be carrying a pocket watch worth a small fortune.

Explosions echo in the distance. The Army is putting dynamite to houses, bringing them down before the flames get their chance. Everyone says it'll stop the spread, because that's what everyone's been told. Yount wishes it would end. Each hollow boom catches in his throat like a clod of tough meat.

Sweat has soaked the menu scrap in his fist—Chicken Jerusalem is an inky smear. He crumples the paper and flings it into the gutter.

The Presidio is bedlam, and San Francisco is still burning.

Humans, spilling out from every tent. Humans, trampling every inch of grass. Mothers keening, toddlers shrieking, old men moaning. Soldiers bark orders into the crowd—orders to conserve water, orders to bury waste. Youngsters play jacks with broken-up twigs and a pinecone. Camp stoves are cold, tempers are hot. Only the bread lines are orderly.

Yount pushes through a clutch of men hauling crates of supplies. There's a high-sour odor coming off their skin and a sickly harmony in their panting breaths. He recalls his time as a patrol officer, nights spent wrangling drunks and hobos, the pitiable sounds they made when he rousted them from their ratholes. Dying-dog sounds. Somewhere between a wheeze and a rattle.

Ellen took great care with his uniform in those days; made sure the blue was free of bloodstains and vomit. He felt sheepish about it. Bad enough for a grown woman to move in with her grown brother, no matter the circumstances, she shouldn't have to wash his dirty things. Morning after his promotion, he gave her money for the laundry around the corner. She said she was happy for the money, but happier for his title. Detective Yount. Her brother, the investigator. Farewell, wharf-bums, goodbye, small potatoes. Big crimes only, forever and ever, Amen.

If Ellen could see him now.

Yount approaches a staff sergeant and presents his badge.

"I'm looking for a woman—"

The man glances at the cardboard, waves it away.

"Don't need that. Don't care. Look all you want."

"I could really use some assistance, looking for this woman in particular."

"Assistance? Nearly everyone here's looking for somebody else. I suggest you get to searching while the light's still good."

Yount runs his hands up his cheeks—stubble scrapes his palms.

"Her name is Bettie. She's young. Missing a pinkie. Port-wine stain on her forehead."

The sergeant's eyes widen.

"Port-wine stain?"

"Yes."

"Right above her eyebrow?" He points at his own.

"Possibly, yes."

"Your wife? Family?"

"No, she's a thief. Stole a pocket watch."

Contempt ripples across the sergeant's face.

"Let's see that little paper of yours again."

Yount passes it over. The sergeant draws his index finger across the chief's signature—gives it a sharp rap.

"Some case they got you on," he says. "Some case. Seems to me you boys would be better served putting out the fires than running around after a piece of jewelry."

Yount is silent.

"Behind the barracks. Plenty of them back there—more every day. Hope you don't mind the smell. Some've been resting for a bit."

"That's where you saw her?"

The sergeant taps the temporary badge against the side of his nose.

"I'll keep this," he says. "Souvenir of a great wrong righted. Here I was, thinking this week was nothing but calamity, but you come along to show me the law's still hard at work, protecting us all. Thank you, detective. You're a real light in the darkness."

The bodies are stacked like kindling, and San Francisco is still burning.

Charred bodies on the top layers, battered bodies underneath. Yount pauses for the dozenth time. He's glad now for the two scant bites of bread rattling around his stomach—less to expel, if it comes to that. The corpse-stench is profound. Rancid meat warmed over. It clings to his hands, saturates his clothes, worms into his nostrils.

For once, he longs for the smoke.

He steels himself and dives back in: raising dead arms, shifting dead torsos, tilting dead heads. Hairs slide under his fingernails. Skin sloughs away at his touch. Less blood than he expected, among all the cadavers, but more bone—sublimely white. Distressingly white.

He remembers Ellen's skull.

There wasn't time, once the earthquake started—not for Yount, not for anything but lurching out of his room and staggering down the hallway, buffeted from side to side. The floorboards snapped and buckled. The electric lights popped. His body was a stranger, moving left when he willed it right, down when he ordered it up. Nothing to hold onto but air. Nowhere to go but forward.

Ellen was alive when he reached the kitchen—alive and gripping the far doorway, even as the walls undulated inward, spitting flour and spices and pans and crockery—alive, until the ceiling cracked open like an egg, and a cast-iron stove dropped through. It caved in the side of her head.

The upstairs neighbor's breakfast—fried apples, thick-cut bacon—splattered her dress.

Her brains splattered the floor.

Their apartment shook for another thirty seconds. Yount was on his hands and knees, shouting her name, when he felt hands grabbing his shoulders, pulling his jacket, dragging him down the stairs and into the street, just as the building began to collapse.

The fires began soon after.

Yount heaves another cadaver.

And another.

And another.

And—

Ice crackles through his chest: Bettie is here. Young, missing pinkie finger, port-wine stain on her forehead, right above the eyebrow. Her tweed skirt is bunched up, caught on her exposed left femur—he lowers it, gingerly.

He checks, of course. He checks because he has to. He checks because it's his job, the one he always wanted, the plump orange carrot that got him through six years of the beat, because the chief will send him packing tomorrow if he comes up empty handed today, because Ellen was proud when he made detective, so proud and so happy, and even after all the hours she spent cleaning his uniforms and cooking his meals and listening to him talk and talk and talk, he can't recall a single goddamn time when he thanked her for a single goddamn thing.

And now she's dead.

So, he checks.

Yes—somehow—Hardesty's watch is still in Bettie's pocket.

The winds have shifted, and San Francisco is still burning.

Yount squints up at the mulberry-red sky. Heat whispers across his face; it's a summery sensation, almost pleasant. The hotel across the street—which is, for the moment, the only open hotel in the city—buzzes with activity. Bellhops and maids and stewards and guests pour in and out of the lobby, carting furniture and toting luggage and wringing hands. No Chicken Jerusalem on the menu tonight, if it ever was. No pillows, goose down or otherwise. Army men are already on their way, wagons loaded with dynamite, for all the good dynamite will do. The flames are coming eventually.

Hardesty's eyes gleam as he strides out of the hotel's front door. He slices through the bustle like a penknife—never elbowed, never shoved—and moves toward Yount with an extended arm.

"Finally! Finally!"

His nose wrinkles when he gets within a few feet of the detective. The arm drops.

"Good Lord," he says. "The reek of you."

"Yes."

"The manager called for me when you arrived. Can you believe the state of this place? Total evacuation, barely an hour's notice. Fire's changed course, apparently, but all this rush-rush-rush; very inconvenient. Exhausting."

Yount gazes at the man. There's a roar behind his eardrums. He can feel the ebb of his veins, the flow of his arteries, his own heart ripping him out to sea.

"Frankly," Hardesty says, "your timing couldn't be better. I met a gentleman earlier—Charles Danvers, good Beacon Hill stock. He has an intimate connection with the railroad. Expects to be heading back east by nine o'clock, and he's guaranteed me a space in his compartment."

"Happy for you."

"Yes, yes."

Hardesty coughs into his knuckles—pats his lapel.

"Well. I understand you have my watch?"

"I do."

"Well."

Yount pulls it from his jacket—the metal is warm.

"Here it is," he says. "I found it at the Presidio, along with Bettie's body."

"Well!"

"I'll make sure all the details are included in my report. Do you have anything else to add, Mr. Hardesty?"

"To your report? Surely not."

"Not to the report, just anything. Anything at all."

Hardesty waves his hand.

"I am grateful for your efforts," he says, "unhurried as they may be."

He holds out an upturned palm.

Yount hurls the pocket watch onto the sidewalk and smashes it with his shoe. He stomps, and stomps, and stomps. He stomps until the eighteen-karat yellow gold folds and twists, soft dough beneath his heel. He stomps until the sapphire inlay shatters; he stomps until the clockwork splinters. He stomps until those splinters are pulverized, little more than dust. He stomps until his ash-baked eyes water and sooty mucus drips from his nose. He stomps until he sees the curve of Bettie's femur, the slope of Ellen's skull. He stomps until the blue-uniformed patrolmen drag him away, screaming, into the smoky night.

San Francisco is still burning.

About the Author

RACHEL HENDERSON lives in New Orleans, where she spends her free time writing and playing bagpipes. Most of her fiction leans toward horror – but, as a once-upon-a-time history major, she also adores exploring historical fiction.

Her stories have appeared in *Hiding Under the Leaves, (s)crawl, foofaraw, After Happy Hour Review, 100-Foot Crow, Neither Fish Nor Foul,* the Creepy podcast, and elsewhere. In 2021, she won first place in the NYC Midnight Short Screenplay Competition. Find her at www.rlhendie.com.

Lucky

Zena Ryder

I'M LUCKY I'M ALIVE. That's what everybody says, anyway. I get that. I heard them same stories as every other soldier. Lose a hand or foot—chances are you'll pull through. Arm above the elbow, or leg above the knee, like me—don't bet on it. I don't feel so lucky right now though. I didn't do nothing to help the Union. But today I'll be leaving this here little tent, leaving you and the other nurses, and then you'll have these two cots for a couple more broken soldiers. I'll be going back home to Chestnut Hill and nobody needs me moping around, feeling sorry for meself. Ma and Susannah will need me in good spirits.

No, Susannah's not my sweetheart. She's my sister. I'm the youngest. Susannah in the middle. Then John. He was always good to me. After Pa died it was John who worked and gave Ma money for the housekeeping. He's the one who give me piggybacks up the stairs when I was little, afore Ma tucked me into bed, pulling the quilt tight around my feet how I liked it, and kissing me on my forehead, my nose, my mouth. I don't hardly remember missing my Pa because John was always taking care of me and Susannah.

You remind me of her, you know. Same height. Same dark curls. Me, I got my Pa's pale, freckled skin and scraggly, orange mop. But Susannah and John, they got our Ma's complexion and thick, black hair. John was so handsome. I could see that, even when I was a boy. He was tall and strong as a dray horse. Sharp as a sickle too. He always come top, or nearly top anyways, in his class—even though he worked in the paper mill every night after school and most mornings, he helped out on our neighbor Putnam's farm. I sometimes heard him creeping out of the house while it were still dark and shutting the door real gentle, and I was thankful to snug down under my covers and go back to sleep.

When he was still a boy, he decided he would go into lawyering. Said he'd never be short of money to take care of me and Ma and Susannah if he went into the law. Said people was always fighting each other and needing the law to sort things out. When he was done common school, he started studying them big law books and got a clerkship with old lawyer Berkeley over in Germantown. But then the war come and Mr. Lincoln put out the call. John said he was going to enlist and lick some damn rebels. Wanted to fight for the Union. Said it'd be dishonorable not to.

I always wanted to do what John did. He said he had to go. Well, if John had to go, I had to go. John never had no trouble telling right from wrong. I thought that would have made him a good lawyer. I sometimes got confused about what was right and wrong—like telling Ma she looked nice in her new poke bonnet when really it looked like she had her head stuck in a coal scuttle. But John weren't never confused. So when he signed up, I did too. I know I look like a boy. Can't never grow much in the way of whiskers. But I was of an age to join, just barely. John acted so proud of me. Clapped his hand on my shoulder. Said I was a man. We walked home that day feeling like giants, like we was doing something that mattered. Something we'd tell our own sons with pride. And let me tell you, I felt like a man that day, remembering the feel of my brother's hand on my shoulder.

Our Ma, oh how she wept. And then I got that confused feeling. It was right to sign up, but it was wrong to make Ma so sad. Which maybe meant it weren't right to go after all. But then we wouldn't be doing our duty to our country. Susannah, though, she weren't sad. At least not then. She were right furious. She flew at John in a rage, thumping on his chest with her fists. She loved him, just like I did, but she said she'd never forgive him if he got hisself or me killed.

But John, he listened to our womenfolk, comforted them as best he could, but said he couldn't live with hisself if he sat out the war. Wouldn't be a man if he didn't fight like other men. Ma and Susannah didn't set much stock by what John was saying, but I did. God forgive me but I felt resentment towards them at that moment, wanting to keep me a child and not be a man who could cut his own meat. And when John said I'd made up my own mind to go, without no persuasion from him, that I knew my own mind, well, right then, I felt like my brother and me, we was invincible. You seen enough wounded men to know how stupid that were. But John said he'd look out for me when we got to the war and I thought with God and John looking out for me, Ma and Susannah would see us come home as heroes after the war was done and the rebels was beat. Do you know, I don't think the possibility of never coming home, never seeing Ma and Susannah again, I don't think it entered my thick skull. And I don't think it entered John's neither.

But what you think war is before you go—ha! Mostly, war's a lot of too-cold or too-hot and damp and sickness and waiting and marching and gnawing hardtack. But a battle's something else. If you never been in one, you can't imagine what it's like. You picture the armies in their bright, clean uniforms and shiny buckles, lined up across a grassy field, firing their rifles at each other, and it's clear who's who and the ones who can stand the longest, who bravely move forward into the enemy's fire, well they're who wins and the enemy runs off with their tails between their legs.

But it weren't like that at all. It was so smoky from all the rifles and from the shells and the trees that was burning, and the bushes burning, even though the ground was wet and muddy and stuck to our brogans in great clods. And the noise. You wouldn't believe the noise. We couldn't see in the smoke and there was horses screaming and cannons booming and rifle fire all around us and the deafening cracking noise of burning wood.

John and me, we got separated from our platoon. Our first battle it was. We was all turned round and couldn't tell which way was the enemy and which was back to our own lines. So we took stock. Didn't move, just hunkered down in the hollow of a big old tree, that smelled of skunk and rotten leaves. John put his arm round me. It was cramped in that hollow with our Springfields and cartridge boxes, canteens and knapsacks. Back home, he'd said he'd take care of me, and he was. I wasn't thinking straight. John said it was sensible not to rush ahead, maybe the wrong way. But then I heard our captain yelling, not ten yards from us. He was ordering our platoon to press forward. I started up and I could just make him out through the smoke, could see which way he was headed with some of the other boys from our platoon. I saw my pal, Bill, and the Wallace boy who'd wet hisself when we first charged. But there Wallace was, shoulder to shoulder with our captain, redeeming hisself. There was about ten of them, maybe a dozen, that I could see, that's all. I tried to move forward onto my knees, but John pressed on my shoulder.

—But, John, I told him, I can see which way to go now. I see our boys heading thataway. John told me to shush. Said we got lucky and found ourselves a safe spot and we could wait this one out. I told him he didn't need to worry about me, I didn't need protecting, that I could fight like Bill, who loved shooting at rebs like they was squirrels.

—Come on, John, I said. Let's go. We gotta go. It was dark, but I could see his eyes glistening. The smoke did sting my eyes too. I got to my knees, ready to duck out of our hole. But John didn't move. He hung on to my sleeve. Inside that old tree, I could smell his sweat and mine and the damp wool of our coats, along with the skunk smell. That hollow surrounded by all that smoke and fire and shells shrieking over our heads. His fingers gripped the cloth of my jacket.

—Stay, he said. I'll look after you. You're safe here. I looked at John and it was like nothing I ever knowed was real. Like maybe not even trees and pots and pans and dogs and horses. Like I couldn't trust nothing I ever thought was true. And the shame of it is that I wanted to sink back under his arm, back into the hollow of that tree. Close my eyes and try not to hear the screaming and shouting and rifle fire. Try not to smell the powder and smoke and blood. But Bill was real close, yelling about damn rebs and how many there was, like fleas on a dog. I heard someone else moaning, like in pain. I don't know who it was, but they was real close too.

Them voices made me yank my arm away and duck out of the hollow. Trees and brush was on fire, roaring and cracking, men shouting, the air hot and smoky and sharp and it hurt to breathe. I turned back towards the tree. John didn't come out.

After that, I don't remember nothing. I woke up behind the lines, my leg sawed off and burns on my hands and face. I never knowed anything could hurt so bad. I kept wanting to get up off this here cot to go find John. But I couldn't hardly move. I throwed up just trying to get to sitting. I know you cleaned far worse, but I'm sorry for the trouble anyways. They brought in a man with his head all bandaged up and put him on that other cot. At first I thought it was John they brought in, but it weren't. That man were gone the next morning, just spots of his blood left on the pillow, then that and all the sheets was gone too. I could bear anything if I knowed John was alright.

Then they told me John was killed. I didn't believe it at first. John was always so strong and big. I couldn't fathom him being dead. He took care of all of us. I wanted to see him, but they wouldn't let me. I heard Bill outside the tent whispering to Wallace they found John all in bits and pieces. They didn't say nothing about the tree, so maybe they didn't know that part. I reckon a shell must of hit direct on that tree. Our captain said I should remember John how he was in life. But how's that? My memories are all maimed and infected by them last minutes.

When I get home, I'll take care of Ma and Susannah. Since you been giving me laudanum on the regular, the pain's not so bad. I'm sure I'll be able to get work in the paper mill. If not, in Thorp's woolen mill. I'll be dashing about on one leg in no time at all, sure as eggs is eggs.

I'm sorry. I'm all right now. I can't be blubbing like a goddamn baby. I wish I'd got blown to bits with John. But I didn't and now I got to go home with this stump you cleaned and bandaged again and again, and face Ma and Susannah. And I'm not a hero, never even fired one shot at the enemy, and neither is John. They'll ask me how he died, and Ma will believe whatever I tell her. Even though she probably wouldn't think no less of him, I can't tell her what happened. But Susannah. She'll see through it. Always does. She'll get the truth out of me. She said she'd never forgive him if he got hisself killed, and she won't.

At least she'll have the comfort of her memories. She won't think no less of John for what happened. But I do. I can't help it.

When my memories creep up on me, I get that comfort feeling first. John was truly the best brother. But then I think on what happened, and that feeling bleeds away and I'm ashamed for admiring him, and then I'm ashamed for wishing I still could. He's not who I thought he was. I didn't ever really know him after all. But I'm no better than John. Never was. I wanted to stay in that hollow with John's arm round me. I only come out because I was scared. Scared of one of our boys finding me hiding like a lily-liver. I was more scared of that than I was of bullets and balls.

If that tree hollow hadn't been in that spot, John and I wouldn't have had a choice. We would have joined our platoon and done our duty like the others. Instead, it was rotten luck that damn tree was there. The seedling didn't get et by a rabbit, nor sapling destroyed by a deer, got enough rain and sun to grow big enough to hide two men in the middle of a battle. And it's no comfort to wonder how many men hailed for their bravery would have hidden inside a hollow had one presented itself, and they was merely lucky it did not.

About the Author

ZENA RYDER is a Brit living in BC, Canada, writing historical fiction mostly set during the American Civil War. She's currently querying agents with a novel about a young woman committed to an insane asylum during the War. At the same time, she's working on her next novel, which is about an 'old maid' who became a Union spymaster while living in the Confederate capital. Zena's run an in-person writing group since 2018 and is founding the First Novel Fellowship, an online community for people who want to write the first draft of their first novel in one year.

Body #311

Christopher DeWitt

CONSTABLE BOYLE'S HANDS FUMBLED on the last button on his coat when the door to his little office clattered open. He was not used to being startled in his quiet little office in this quiet little Irish town, and it annoyed him not a little.

When he saw the look on the man's face as he entered, he bit back the acerbic comment forming at the back of his throat. He knew that he had been ill of late, after all.

"Mr. Druery," he said shortly by way of greeting, his hand quickly fastening that last button into place. *That will fix me for violating my own fastidious rule*, he thought: Always wear your officer coat properly while on duty.

The constable studied John Druery carefully, noting that he clutched a newspaper fiercely in one hand—*WAY TIMES* he could read just above the fold. *June 16, 1915* beneath it.

Mr. Druery's eyes had not left his since he had entered the office. The clock ticked on dutifully, the only sound filling the space for the moment.

"I'll need to use your telephone, please." Mr. Druery's voice was somber and steady. He stepped a little further into the light offered by the office window at this early hour. Boyle worked to maintain a steady demeanor, now seeing the haunted expression on Mr. Druery's features.

Boyle straightened up a little, drawing in a breath. "I'm sorry, Mr. Druery," he began, regaining his officiousness. "As you know, it's only to be used for official business." The constable leaned forward and pressed the knuckles of both of his fists on the surface of his desk to emphasize his point. "There's a war on, you know," he smirked.

Mr. Druery stared at him.

"I am sorry," Boyle murmured, then cleared his throat. The entire town knew that Constable Boyle was a stickler for regulation.

"I fear this is official business, Constable Boyle." Mr. Druery's voice was soft, but it somehow rang like a clarion for Boyle. "I fear this is war business."

Mr. Druery laid the paper on the desktop.

"I must contact the Cunard Line." He pronounced it Kyunard, in the British fashion. Constable Boyle's belly tightened at the name of the shipping line. Druery's uttering it could mean only one thing. Everyone knew it. It was on everyone's minds, everyone's lips these days.

"Of course, John, of course," Boyle managed, his mouth suddenly dry. The soles of his shoes scraped loudly on the old stone floor as he stepped aside, his arm sweeping grandly, toward the telephone on his desk. "You may'nt reach them directly. You'll have to go through the exchange."

"Yes," said Mr. Druery simply, gently tapping the receiver to raise the operator.

Boyle started to say something, his curiosity getting the better of him. There was an audible click when he quickly closed his mouth, and he cursed himself.

Mr. Druery was half-turned from him, but his head moved slightly, indicating he had heard it. "Yes, Constable Boyle, it's her." Boyle stepped back slightly, involuntarily. "It's Maeve."

"Dear me," Boyle said softly. "Dear me, no."

A tiny, imploring voice drifted up to the two men. Mr. Druery cleared his throat and spoke into the telephone's mouthpiece.

Maeve Druery stared across the smooth, almost glassy surface of the Celtic Sea. It was a clear day, clearer and brighter than usual according to what she overheard from the ship's crew. Still, she was glad to have the coat her parents had given her when she had departed for the States. One hand absently played with one of the coat's buttons; it had become something of a habit. She loved the buttons of the coat most of all, large and brass and embossed with the image of a large legendary bird just rising from flames threatening to devour it.

The coast of Ireland was a firm, distant emerald. Her parents were there, waiting for her. Enjoying this beautiful, early day in May should have helped erase any doubt as to what she had done, this extraordinary move to leave a good situation in America, a good job, the prospects of at least two fine gentlemen courting her. A new life, budding with hope. And yet here she was, returning to her old one. She had hoped the anticipation of surprising her Ma and Da with an early return would take the sting from all of that, but it really hadn't.

Mr. Howard, her employer in New Jersey, had been too kind when she had abruptly announced that she was leaving his employ to return to Ireland.

"Well, we Americans are not to everyone's taste, to be sure," he joked, hiding his disappointment in his amiable way. "The kids will miss you, I'm sure, but they'll understand, in time."

And she would miss the kids, too, Maeve thought. Kenneth with his endless fascination with machines, Virginia and her infectious giggle and glorious curls, Little Andy with his particular talent for getting more food on his clothes than in his mouth. All darling children in a comfortable home, with kind, thoughtful parents. A nanny could not have asked for better. Maeve knew just how fortunate she had been.

"Yes, Mr. Howard, I have no doubt of that." She couldn't believe she was saying the words out loud, though she had rehearsed them enough. "But my parents, you see... Da has been ill and Ma is getting up there in age. The inn's just too much for them now. Ma sent me a letter, asking me back."

"Family is so important," Mrs. Howard had interjected earnestly. "Believe me, we understand that." Her lovely green eyes had glistened with emotion. "Besides, who's to say you won't return to us one day?"

Maeve had simply nodded, looking down, swallowing back a tiny sob.

An exclamation from one of the ship's crew nearby wrenched her from her thoughts, the voice having a bluntly curious, slightly alarmed quality to it, as if an old friend of theirs had shown up unexpectedly.

Maeve's attention was immediately drawn to a distant burbling on the water's surface, some few hundred yards off, but clearly visible on this bright, pristine day. She gazed, fascinated, at the disturbance, an effervescent bubbling, very strange and unexpected on the otherwise calm waters. A dolphin? A whale, perhaps. Maeve didn't know if either were common, or even possible in these waters.

Then she saw it. An unmistakable line in the blue-green water, as straight as could be, as if drawn by Poseidon's own hand, arrowing directly at the ship on which Maeve Druery now stood. The sailor's nearby voices rose with more urgency, more alarm.

Maeve felt herself lifting somehow, buoyant with unreality.

The line in the sea became more pronounced, seemed to elongate faster and faster as it sped its way to the ship's hull.

Her thoughts snapped, unbidden, to the events of just a few nights ago, when Captain Turner suddenly appeared at the ship's talent show, quite unexpectedly and to everyone's surprise, including the crew members present. Everyone knew Captain Turner was not a particularly social man. He was always very sober and serious and did not indulge in such frivolity.

> *Sweet heart, dear heart,*
> *Stars shine from the skies,*
> *There's love in your eyes*
> *When my ship comes sailing home.*

The audience sat in rapt attention for a moment as the last note from the piano faded and was replaced with applause.

Maeve thought the applause tepid at first, even hesitant, but realized it was merely from surprise at how clear and lovely the singer's voice had been. Like that of a professional performer rather than just another passenger on the ship. The woman stood on the stage, her growing smile making her even more radiant. She curtsied with the expert finesse of a veteran entertainer.

The gentleman who had assigned himself the role of master of ceremonies of the ad hoc talent show took to the stage, applauding and beaming a grin as if he had something to do with the woman's performance.

A nervous twinge clutched at Maeve's stomach, suddenly doubting the wisdom of performing her own song.

"But you must do it, Maevey." Maeve felt a hand on her arm. It was Polly, her cabin mate whom she had befriended during the voyage. "I can see that you are nervous, silly goose..." Polly stood, tugging at Maeve's hand.

"No, really, Polly, I couldn't. Not after that." She let out a humorless chuckle.

"Really, now. You—"

The last of the applause dwindled and all movement in the room seemed to stop at once, save for the uniformed man entering through the main doors. A few men from the ship's crew stood and turned respectfully to him, one immediately dousing a cigarette in the ashtray near him.

"Pardon, ladies and gentlemen, I did not mean to interrupt," the man said, his voice an impressive baritone. He looked about the room, a quick, polite smile crossing his face. He was an older man, and to Maeve it was evident he was a man used to deference paid by other men. He had an immediate, commanding presence. He looked about the room again, as if assessing all who were there, his expression intense and serious.

"Trust that I won't be long, please." A palpable, expectant hush fell across the room, the only sound, distant and always present, was the constant thrumming of the ship's engines. "I know that there has been much discussion on board about the reported threat of a U-boat attack among passengers and, sad to say, crew." Here he threw a baleful eye at the purser, the man who had put out his cigarette. The purser looked quickly down and away. There was a collective, quiet gasp from the audience. Someone chuckled nervously. "Yes, yes. We have all at least heard of the warning the German navy posted in the papers."

"Oh yes, Captain. We have been warned!" the master of ceremonies called out with a jaunty wave of his hand, the smoke of the cigar he held in it wafting momentarily in the air above him.

Captain Turner stared at the man, clearly not amused. The master of ceremonies shrugged slightly and tapped the cigar, sullying the crystal ashtray on the piano.

"I want to assure you," The captain continued, "that the hoisting of the lifeboats to their extended positions is entirely routine. Also, there have been no reports of U-boat activity in this area. In any case, this vessel's capability of outpacing the speed of any U-boat is, as you know, unmatched."

The room remained still as the captain further surveyed his passengers.

"Please excuse me and enjoy the remainder of your evening." The captain turned on his heel and departed the room.

"Well," Polly said, letting out a breath. "Are we sufficiently reassured?"

Maeve wasn't entirely sure that she was.

Maeve blinked away the memory of that evening, her eyes snapping again to the razor-straight blue-green line drawing itself inexorably closer, as undaunted as the sea itself. The ship and ship's crew were strangely quiet, almost placid, as this perfect line in the sea, the one that did not truly belong there, not made by God, or Poseidon but only Fate, arrowed through the sea at them, unstoppable.

Maeve lost the blue-green line now, the hull of the ship blocking its progress from her view. She drew in a breath and a suffocating silence enveloped her in its gauzy cocoon. Then there was nothing. Had it missed? Somehow gone beneath the ship?

Everything slowed down in that instant. It started as a slight shudder at her feet. She looked down, almost expecting the polished wood of the deck to shatter that very moment. The shudder became a jarring rattle. She staggered, her knees meeting the deck with a sharp, jolting pain.

Something then rose up in front of her, an unreal wall of something white and terrifying, towering over the deck. It tore a lifeboat from its davits, blasting it to atoms, its hull instantly transformed to splinters showering around her.

The ship moved through the white wall as it even then started to come down on the vessel, the sea's water powerfully descending, soaking crew, passengers, deck. Then came more debris, this time steel, the wounded ship's skin coming down in shards, rivets pelting down like deadly rain.

Maeve hunkered down, one hand grasping the deck rail, amazed that no one had been struck or injured by the storm of debris. Maeve felt the ship move abruptly, straying from its original course, lurching to starboard, where the torpedo had struck, a significant roll and dip at the bow.

My God, she thought. *Torpedo. It's happened. It's actually happened.* She was living a nightmare, one that had, up until this moment resided in the back of all the passenger's minds. But here it was.

The ship continued to move forward, the bow appearing to reach for the shore, for Old Head of Kinsale, looking to Maeve's eye unbearably distant, but also seeming to beckon like ancient sirens.

Passengers began filling the boat deck, looking quizzically about at the fallen debris, a soft gabble of questions and subtly alarmed voices starting to fill the air.

A ship's officer carefully and politely made his way through the growing surge of people, raising his voice over the clamor.

"The ship will be alright, do not worry, ladies and gentlemen! We will be alright! The ship is sound…" He continued forward along the boat deck repeating the comforting message. Crew members quietly manned the winches at the lifeboat stations. Maeve noticed an uncertain look pass between them.

Hoisting out the lifeboats is routine, Captain Turner's words echoed Maeve's mind. Her throat felt like it was filled with cotton. Her pulse quickened.

A gentleman emerged from a hatchway; his arms filled with lifejackets. He began handing them out randomly. Maeve reached out to take one. She had no idea how to put it on.

"Remember how we had gone through these. The instructions are posted in your cabins," the gentleman said, as if reading her thoughts. Maeve did not remember ever being drilled on the use of the lifejackets. She then recalled only glancing at the instructions, posted on the inside of the cabin door. The only thing that stood out to her at the time was that they were called Boddy life jackets. She had found it darkly amusing at the time. What good would instructions in the cabins do now?

She watched as one man started to put one on, straps flying awkwardly this way and that. It already did not look right to her. She set to work donning her own, hoping for the best.

The crewmen were trying to keep passengers orderly as they climbed into the boats. Maeve felt that a surge of panic was starting to develop in the crowd as the ship heeled further. She concentrated on taking deep, steady breaths, to check her own rising panic.

She looked about for Polly, a familiar face to help comfort her. She took a few steps closer to the nearest lifeboat. It looked somehow bigger now, but only half-filled with people. Her eyes connected with a woman in the boat, her arms drawn tightly about her, face shockingly white, eyes wide as saucers, shining with fear and apprehension. Maeve smiled at her, with a reassurance she herself did not feel. The woman looked away then, her face falling to a sad disappointment.

"Here now," said a handsome, tanned sailor, reaching out to Maeve, his eyes cast downward. She reached to him, then realized he was looking at the widening gap between the lifeboat and the ship's hull. The sea's surface lay sixty feet below, no longer calm, no longer beautiful. She held back, her arm stiffening. The sailor looked up at her, a confident grin making him handsomer still. "It'll be alright, miss. Almost there."

She stepped into the boat, looking about for a place to sit. "Here you go, dear," a matronly woman announced, patting an empty space on the boat's thwart beside her. "Plenty of room for a slight lass like yourself."

Maeve smiled graciously, sitting down opposite of the woman who she had had earlier exchanged glances. The woman gazed at her again, this time with more intensity, her eyes shining again with tears. She reached over and took Maeve's hands into hers.

"Thank you, miss," she said. Maeve nodded and squeezed her hands in return.

Suddenly, the boat lurched downward. Maeve felt herself raise up off the thwart, a momentary dizzying sensation. The boat ceased its downward motion as abruptly. One of the crewmen cursed loudly. There was a clanking at the winch. Maeve heard a muttered "Sorry, mum."

The boat resumed its downward journey. Maeve saw a man in the bow fiddling with his lifejacket. She was convinced it was upside down. She opened her mouth to say something to him, but a shout burst from the boat deck, quickly followed by a flurry of commotion. "Hey there!" Arms grasped out to attempt to stop a boy as he ran and hurled himself from the ship. A man half-caught the boy as he sprawled into the lifeboat, narrowly missing most of the passengers in his path, but knocking a young man nearly over the side.

"Damn you!" The man who had caught him growled. "You might have killed yourself, boy! What if you had missed??"

The lad looked up at Maeve, red-faced. "Pop made me," he gusted out, his breath hot. "I'm sorry." He looked up at the boat deck, moving upward, further away from the lifeboat, with each screech of the winches. A man peered over the rail at the boy, an anguished grimace twisting his features.

The blocks squealed, the ropes racing through them, the boat lowering agonizingly slowly, cast in the shadow of the towering ship, smoke still billowing dutifully from its stacks, though the engines had slowed to allow for the lifeboats to be deployed.

The lifeboat lurched again, bow down, the screeching of the ropes halted for a breathless moment, then began racing ever faster, the bow swinging down quickly, alarmingly.

Maeve fell. There was a moment of intense silence, her mind scrabbling with this new danger. Then dark coldness as the sea embraced her. She involuntarily opened her eyes in her fright, watched as the others from the lifeboat tumbled in, the surface churning above them, silhouetted against the relatively illuminated surface.

Maeve grasped at her lifejacket, suddenly afraid it might somehow float off from her body, not properly strapped after all. The jacket was doing its job instead. She was floating upward, to life, to the sunny air. At last, she broke through the surface, gasping, drinking in the blessed oxygen, people all around her doing the same, shouting, screaming, crying. Men yelling from above, "Clear the ship! Please move away! We are lowering more boats! Clear the way!"

Maeve looked down the vast length of the vessel. Indeed, other boats were being lowered, but more people were jumping, trying to leap the gap from the ship to the lifeboat, many not making it, falling into the sea, arms and legs flailing awfully. Some gawked from the rail, too afraid to do anything but watch, others from the boats peered upward at those they left behind, still on the ship, arms reaching, hands grasping in futility.

A loud snapping sound tore through the calamity. A lifeboat crashed onto one already on the surface Maeve flinched, her gaze in that instant isolated on an old man being crushed before her eyes, his head obliterated by the boat's hull.

Maeve gulped more air, closing her eyes tightly against the horror, chest heaving.

"Clear away, damn you!" she heard again from above. She realized she was moving away from it all, drifting, the current pulling her, the ship's wake diminished but still pushing her. Lifeboats were making it intact to the surface, most half-full of passengers, some men inexpertly manning oars, others trying to pull people from the water.

Maeve spotted a pink cap with a fanciful feather sprouting incongruously from it.

Polly! It had to be Polly!

They had unpacked together in their cabin, and Polly had excitedly opened her hat box. "You have to see this, Maevy!" She was already calling her "Maevy" even though they had only just met. "It's a Georgette! I spent almost a whole paycheck on it, but I think it's worth it. Don't you?" It was the first thing she had unpacked.

Maeve raised a hand, waving it frantically above her head. "Polly! Polly, over here!"

The white oval of Polly's face looked about, the outlandish feather wagging with the movement.

"Oh, Polly!" Meave laughed a little despite herself, a little hope rising within her. "You and that silly hat!"

But Polly's attention had been diverted elsewhere. A man was moving her more inboard so he could better help people in the water.

"Here! Polly, here!" Maeve called again, her voice weaker, almost choking on the last syllable. She looked to her right. A man's legs jutted oddly upward from the water, as if he were diving like an oversized seabird. His legs were not moving at all. She shifted her gaze around her, seeing others just like it. It would have been funny if not so horrific. These people had drowned, their Boddy lifejackets not having been put on properly.

Hands shaking, Maeve again checked the clips and straps of her own lifejacket.

Only then did Maeve realize how thirsty she had become, one hand involuntarily going to her throat.

"Help!" she croaked, her voice already so very faint. The tragi-comic upside-down bodies drifted mercifully further from her. She looked again for Polly's boat. The surface of the sea was starting to crowd her visibility. She could still see the stern of the ship, angling down sickeningly, tiny people still clinging to it.

She could hear a muted, yet thunderous groan as the last of the vessel slipped under. The people in the boats and in the water seemed to cry as one, blending with the din of the ship's last moment. Then there was an eerie, funereal silence as the survivors gaped at the emptiness of the sea.

Maeve stared, not believing it was already gone. She could see nothing but sea, a few seabirds, and sky.

She turned her head slightly, searching, her hand reaching up, fiddling with the large brass button of her coat.

There it was. The sliver of land seen earlier, still marginally within sight, not ten or twelve miles off. Old Head of Kinsale. Ireland.

"I will see you soon, Ma… Da…" she said to the sea. For surely someone would find her, ever so close to land, this close to home, on this clear bright day on the Celtic Sea.

"Thank you for arriving so quickly, Mr. Druery."

John Druery looked at the Cunard Line man, eyes solemn. "Of course."

"I'm Selkirk, with Cunard Line," said the man, shaking Mr. Druery's hand. Mr. Druery waited silently as Selkirk took a deep breath and reached for a file on his desk.

"Mrs. Druery?" he said hesitantly.

"She doesn't need to see this."

"I see," Selkirk said softly, "Indeed. You must understand, Mr. Druery, the condition of the body—"

"Yes," Mr. Druery's voice was clipped, forceful. He drew himself up, taking a deep breath.

"We've only a photograph, as you know, as the body had to be—"

"Interred. Yes, I understand. And thank you."

Selkirk blinked, his mouth tightening. He nodded curtly. He picked up the file, unwinding the string fastener. The clatter of footsteps from the hall outside the office drifted in, the distant, murmured conversation of two men. He took the photograph out of the file and placed it gently on the desktop, swiveled it around for Mr. Druery with his fingertips.

Mr. Druery looked at Selkirk, expression suddenly very frightened. He closed his eyes, as if steeling himself, took a faltering step closer. He put one hand flat on the desktop, tightened the other into a fist, and opened his eyes.

Mr. Druery stared at the photograph. Selkirk could tell he was not breathing. He had witnessed many reactions just like it.

Mr. Druery unclenched his fist and reached out, his hand trembling, turning the photograph over.

"It's her," his voice was a croaking whisper.

Selkirk slowly folded his hands at his waist. "We must be sure, Mr. Druery," he said gently.

"The buttons."

Selkirk stared at John Druery. His hand went to his chin, his eyes carefully studying Mr. Druery's downcast face.

"The coat. It was a parting gift from us when she left for America."

Selkirk reached for the photograph, flipping it back over, away from Mr. Druery. He looked closely at the grotesque image:

#311 had been handwritten on a white card and carefully placed next to the decomposed remains of a woman. She was still wearing a lifejacket. The name of the vessel on the lifejacket was faded but could still be made out.

Lusitania.

What remained of the woman's hand still grasped one of the large buttons of her coat, as if she was still fiddling with it in death.

The brass button was embossed with the image of a bird.

It was a Phoenix rising from the ashes.

Maeve Druery had come home.

On May 5, 1915, Royal Mail Ship *Lusitania* was struck in the starboard bow by a single torpedo launched from German Imperial Navy U-Boat *U-20*. From the moment the torpedo hit to the time of her sinking, 18 minutes had passed.

Of the 1,959 passengers aboard her, only 764 survived. Of

the 33 infants aboard, 6 survived. 791 people were designated as missing. Of that number, only 173 bodies were recovered. As the bodies were recovered, they were assigned numbers and photographed, in the hopes that their families might find some closure, finally learning the fate of their loved ones.

On June 11, 1915, the body of a female, still wearing a Boddy lifejacket marked *Lusitania*, was discovered by the lighthouse keeper on Straw Island, off Galway.

The woman had been adrift for 36 days.

The body was never identified.

About the Author

CHRISTOPHER DEWITT lives in Phoenix, Arizona with his wife Christine, son Alex, three dopey but lovable dogs, and a weird, vegan cat. When he isn't writing and reading, he is exploring the beautiful and sometimes eerie Superstition Mountains and the haunts of Tombstone. He also occupies his free time trying to figure out if his house—built practically on top of old western mines—is as haunted as The Copper Queen Hotel in Bisbee, Arizona (It is!). A United States Air Force veteran and licensed pilot, he loves anything that flies and earth-bound racing machines that go very, very fast.

The Violinist

Ezra Harker Shaw

Berlin,
November 1903

THE CONCERT IS ONLY A FEW HOURS AWAY.

Eva has been practicing since dawn so fitfully and unproductively that she is sure her violin, a Stradivarius named Emiliani, has developed a resentment towards her.

He lies across the chaise-lounge of the Berlin hotel room, his back turned with the particular insouciance and hubris of a wounded aristocrat.

He is worth something, the slender hunch of his shoulders seems to say; he was crafted by Antonio Stradivari himself, cradled by the brilliance of Ludwig Strauss, passed through years in the hands of Eva's teacher, and until now has always been praised and petted, revered for his brilliance; and yet now, somehow, he is being battered by a frightened amateur.

"Once more?" she asks, her hands trembling with self-loathing. "If we could just try once more, I'm sure we could perfect that phrase."

As she lifts him by the neck she feels the weight of his resistance. "Remember how well we played it for Edvard Grieg? Wasn't that wonderful?"

It was a fluke, the voice in her head tells her the violin is muttering.

"Perhaps," she says aloud, her voice low and reassuring,

"but perhaps we can conjure another fluke."

Emiliani is skeptical.

It is only one passage in Paganini's Caprice that she struggles with, and if she were more generous to herself, Eva would note that in her twenty years of performing (which include seventeen recitals of the Caprice) she has never once made an error on stage.

She raises the violin to her chin, holds the bow aloft, and for a moment the world inhales around them; and then, the offending section—a furious flurry of notes that sends her scuttling up and down the neck between positions, her fingers jumping about at frantic speed, leaping out of each other's way and, inevitably, crashing into each other, tangling and sending the notes ricocheting off at the wrong pitch and in the wrong direction.

Emiliani screeches, sends the bow flying away with a kick of displeasure. Eva staggers back, breath scraping at her sternum, strangling her throat, and she fights the panic that has already settled in her heart.

Dropping Emiliani back onto the chaise-lounge, never mind if he is a Stradivarius, Eva staggers to the hotel room window, her shaking fingers struggling with the latch until she gets it free, and a blast of Berlin winter air slaps her across the face.

The cold comes with the clatter and chatter of the busy street, and she lets her head rest against the lintel, allowing the winter cool to still her hot brain. Up on the first floor, she is above the busy street, looking out on frosted windows and white-capped roofs of Charlottenstraße.

Below, the street bustles with energy: carriages trot and stop, banging and blustering as they maneuver around each other; a motorcar honks, and people shout over the hubbub.

Eva turns her head, searching for the music in her mind. She had it—just the other day she and Bella played the whole thing through with only the smallest imperfections. But one perfect rehearsal, as her teacher drilled into her in childhood, is worth nothing. One has to be able to recreate it at any moment; one has to be ready for performance.

Eva, specifically, has to be ready for performance in about—she glances at the ormolu clock—two hours and forty minutes.

This rehearsal isn't getting anywhere; she can tell that. She knows herself, knows that a rest will help, though finds it difficult to stop. At least Bella will be back soon; she's only gone to Friedrichstraße to look at the department stores.

"Come with me, just this once, you'll enjoy it," Bella had said. "It's good to relax."

"But how on earth is one to relax with one's Paganini in such a mess and the clock relentlessly counting down to the public execution of imperfection?" Eva declined.

She wishes they were back in Paris, where the two of them could go out to a salon or to meet friends in a cafe, where there would be demands upon her time, that might—might—help her forget their impending performance.

Still, she and Bella have performed their duo in Berlin several times and it has never cast such oppression over her nerves before.

Tonight is different, though, she knows that.

He will be there tonight, he has promised. And she will be aware of him, will feel his presence unsettling her. Is he the reason this rehearsal troubles her even more than usual?

Oh, where is Bella? If she were here they could play together, and that would calm Eva's frantic nerves. Bella would talk softly, say things like, "It's no use trying to do finger gymnastics when one is dizzy. Let's play something simple." And together they would draw out the sweet tones of Saint-Saens, gentle tones echoing rich in the small room, and Eva would hear how Emiliani could sing when he was treated kindly, and her heart would rest in andante, grazioso.

She looks out into the street, trying to conjure Bella into the crowd.

Hope lies to her, and twists a middle-aged schoolmistress type into the face of the beloved for half a second, and then disappoints her with the truth. What a foolish mistake, for though that woman is fair, she lacks Bella's marvelous height.

She has a pleasant face though, all the more so when she turns her attention on the two little girls by her side, and Eva finds herself smiling with them. It seemed the woman is agreeing to some treat, for the two little German girls are bouncing on their tip toes in excitement, and she laughs in her generous acquiescence.

Two working men in brown jackets carry a heavy parcel between them, their faces intense with strain, their steps short with caution. The governess pulls the girls back out their way.

All these unfamiliar faces, pink cheeks in thick dark clothes, dull and baffling. Until amongst them a beautiful familiarity, like a lightning flash to her senses, and unmistakable in reality: Bella, tall and fair haired, striding down the street with her customary determination that makes people step out of her way.

Eva leans out, wants to wave, but sees that it would be futile, for Bella's eyes are fixed ahead of her, on earthly matters, not lovers in the heavens. So, abandoning the hope of catching Bella's eye, Eva leaves the window, and calls for tea for two.

Bella Edwards has treated herself with a gift for Eva, and it has put her in a good mood. She hums as she strolls through the shoppers, nodding at strangers with a smile. The evening's music is never far from her thoughts, and sometimes the fingers of her right hand flutter a few bars on the ghost piano of her left sleeve. It will be a good concert, she can feel it already.

As she approaches the hotel where she and Eva are staying, she notices two men carrying between them a block of some apparent weight. One glances at the hotel door and gestures to his fellow with his head, but only very briefly, as if even this small movement is taking away from the effort required for their labor.

She leaps lightly ahead of them, and draws the door open wide.

"Are you coming this way gentlemen?" she enquires in her finest German.

A momentary consternation flashes across their faces, but they mumble their thanks and allow her to hold the door for them.

"What a peculiar parcel!" she says brightly, glancing down at their burden. "You should have brought a cart!"

She is mentally trying to work out what it could be as she leaves them and heads for the staircase, only to hear one of the men say to the clerk a name as familiar as her own. "For Madame Eva Mudocci."

"Madame Mudocci?" she interrupts, before the concierge can consult his records. "That's us. We are on the first floor, if you would oblige us by carrying your burden a little further?"

The younger of the two looks reluctant to lift the package—now set down—for even another minute, but the other nods to him, and between them they hoist up the heavy package once more.

Bella strides ahead of them, waving away the anxious German clerk with no patience for his obsequiences. Soon they find themselves trailing a maid with precarious tea-tray who turns, no less, for Eva and Bella's room.

"It is a busy hour!" Bella calls cheerfully as all four hesitate at the door. "Go on in," she says. "If Eva sent for tea, she'll be ready."

Inside, Eva is waiting; Bella sees the calm nod to the maid, and then the spread of a smile at the sight of Bella, and then the frown of bewilderment at the appearance of the two men.

"We have a most peculiar parcel!" Bella cries over the top of the others, ushering the men in.

Eva processes the situation enough to dart forward and remove a vase from the nearest table, allowing the men to set down their burden.

Bella does wonder if the table can handle this seemingly immense weight, but decides to risk it, dismissing the two carriers and then the maid with polite gratitude, closing the door behind them, and then turning to her Eva.

"Well! What a lot of bustle!"

"What is it?" Eva asks.

Bella rubs her hands to warm them a little before laying one on either side of Eva's waist and delivering a cold kiss to her warm cheek.

"I haven't the faintest idea," she murmurs.

"There's snow in your hair," Eva says fondly. "I saw you coming. I thought you'd be cold so I've ordered some tea."

"Wonderful!"

She gives Eva a last affectionate squeeze and steps away, allowing Eva to investigate the package.

Eva holds her hands up to her chest as she peers down at the paper, as if it were a thing that could reach out. Her dark curls are especially disheveled this afternoon, and there is a tightness to her shoulders that Bella can read as easily as a book.

Of course she is worried about the performance.

Bella shrugs off her coat. "I truly cannot imagine what it is," she says as she puts her coat and hat on the stand by the door. She glances to the mirror as she passes, loosens her blonde hair with a shake and a practiced tousle. She will have to start getting ready soon, she thinks. As a less beautiful woman than Eva, there is less expectation on her to look lovely, but never none. She considers again how easy it might be to go to a new city, cut her hair, and adopt a man's attire (at her height it would be easy to pass), and become Teddie Edwards, devoted pianist to the great Eva Muddoci. Forgo femininity, and be free.

She glances at Eva through the mirror's reflection, and realizes something in her stance has changed. She is unnaturally still, as if something in the parcel has set a petrifaction spell upon her.

"What is it?" Bella asks, coming to her side.

Eva's dark hair falls loose around her face, half hiding the expression, but Bella catches a strained, wild spark in the eyes, and a nervous bite to the lip, and she knows, with an inward groan, what Eva will say before she says it.

"It is from Edvard."

Edvard Munch's handwriting is wobbly and blotched, though he has clearly put in some effort here (she has complained about the illegible scrawl of his letters so many times it has become a sore spot between them). He claims he cannot be contained within the lines of neat script.

Eva's hands are shaking. Part of her is not sure she wants to open it with Bella beside her, for Munch is quite capable of appalling, but the other part of her wants the comfort, the protection even, of Bella's practical calm.

She fumbles at the brown paper that wraps the parcel. Her impression of the dead weight before her is of a tombstone, something huge and silent and heavy, something that will foretell the season of her own mortality and mark her legacy beyond.

One layer within, a small slip of white paper with the same inky, spidery handwriting, less constrained than in the address, seeping out the words:

Here is the stone that fell from my heart.

Pulse pounding in her ears, Eva tears off the last layers, revealing in a moment a stark, beautiful image of herself in black upon a huge white stone.

Munch had shown her his Madonna—voluptuously naked and haloed in a terrifying red; she sees now an echo of that painting in this, but here is her own face, intelligent and thoughtful, surrounded by sensuous waves of hair, and modestly dressed with a great, shining broach at her throat.

The stone is rectangular, rough-hewn around the edges, but perfectly smooth on its face. It has a cold, impressive silence to it that seems to draw in all sound and consume it.

The brooch, she realizes, is the bolesølje she was given in Norway, said to ward off wicked spirits. He admired it when he saw her wearing it, and spoke with pleasure at seeing the artifact from his homeland; he told her that, to protect himself against evil, he keeps her picture above his bed.

She doesn't know whether to be happy or afraid. Whenever they meet, they talk for long, hourless days in clumsy, halting German that neither of them speaks well of cerebral and esoteric matters that are difficult to negotiate even in one's mother tongue.

He believes strange and wonderful things, talks of auras and souls, and sometimes he is skittish and scared, and Eva feels she can confess her imaginative and childish fears, which he not only takes seriously but often amplifies.

All her dreaminess, her wildness and occultism—things she feels half ashamed of—she can express around him, and this, this is how he sees her.

Is this who she is? Is she really so beautiful, so powerful, so magnificent?

This petrification is a miracle, a transformation of imperfect flesh into perfect image, and Eva need never play again.

Bella looks at her love. Some light in her has cloaked itself, retreated to somewhere distant within.

Damn Edvard Munch! Why do men always have to force these relics, these testaments to their affection, upon one?

Eva, with her curly hair, dark-eyed beauty and sensitive nature, is an inevitable draw to such men. Bella is glad she herself is no longer a temptation: too tall, too clever, too inclined to speak her mind when she sees things are ridiculous.

When she was younger, there had been men who'd adored her, Grieg the best and worst of them. He had encouraged her talent, played with her, tutored her on how to perform his works. All that had flattered and brought joy to her as a young pianist, but once he began to pester her to meet in some quiet place, never mind he was thirty years older than her and had a lovely wife, she felt the relationship tainted. Had there been the least physical attraction, it would have been easy to give in, but a man like Grieg had never been her interest.

Besides, though she was flattered by his attentions, she did not need them. Eva is different. Eva is always afraid of her own inadequacy, and always seeking some evidence to counter it.

To be a muse surely offers a rush of reassurance, and when Munch finds the object of his worship too independently willed, he will drop her, regardless of whether she will roll or shatter.

Perhaps Eva craves a life two women can never quite fully have, however their bohemian circle might accept them. And perhaps—Bella has to admit, to acknowledge that little lingering fear—perhaps Eva genuinely likes Edvard Munch: his strange intelligence, his ethereal mysticism, his impulsivity and creativity.

He is everything Bella is not, and while she is happy to be herself, she knows Eva is somewhere between the two of them.

Eva's reverie is finally broken by Bella's voice, unusually loud and somewhat brittle in its cheerfulness.

"I shall acknowledge, that is beautiful, but what on earth are we to do with it?"

The ethereal wanderings her mind had taken are brushed away in this marvelously frank question, and as her love for Bella surges up through her, she shudders into a laugh that is close to tears.

"What are we to do with it?" she echoes. Bella laughs with her, her lovely ironical laugh that twists her mouth. Eva's laugh only grows, until it bends her double and she has to clutch the table.

"We shall take it from town to town," Bella says, the grin on her face showing she is enjoying Eva's laugh even more than her own. "To every hotel and every city on our tour, and we shall place it on the mantelpiece, and we shall break a good many mantelpieces in the process!"

At this, Eva laughs so hard she fears losing control of her bladder and drops entirely to her knees. "Stop, stop!" she cries, trying to wipe at her eyes and subdue the giggles that still wrack her.

Bella shrugs and sends a wicked wink her way. "Very well. I'm frozen, and I'm sure you've been exhausting yourself with rehearsal. Shall we have that tea?"

As she tries to slow her breathing, Eva brings herself back up to standing, putting a hand to her side where a stitch is forming. As she rises above the table, she looks at the stone again. It is still there, and still beautiful.

"Well done, Edvard," she whispers.

Across the room, the china clinks, and the teapot pours. "You know I don't normally care for Herr Munch's work, but I shall acknowledge that this is an exceedingly lovely piece."

Eva nods. Truthfully, she doesn't really like Edvard's work that much either — instead she craves the beauty and precision of the Pre-Raphaelites, or the wildness and splendor of the German Romantics — but she always enjoys how he talked about his art.

"I paint with my soul," he had said, his eyes bulging with excitement and eagerness.

Bella, who had been sitting with them, wistfully commented, "I once played the piano with my soul." She had smiled meekly at Edvard. "It sounded terrible. Now I play with my hands and practice every day so they get better."

Eva had been cross with her later; fortunately poor Edvard had lost the thread of Bella's swift, confident German, and the joke was lost on him.

Now, Bella hands Eva a cup of tea, and pauses to examine the stone critically. "It's a lithograph stone, isn't it? You carve into it, and then use it to print onto paper?"

"I believe so."

"Then why in the name of all the saints didn't he send a print?" Bella said.

Eva feels the laughter rising in her again and sets down her cup. She can see from a tweak in the corner of Bella's mouth that she knows what she is doing.

"Well, at least he's given up trying to paint you," Bella says. "That ghastly portrait where you looked like a ghoul... all that strange darkness behind you. It was horrible."

"Yes." Eva instantly recollects a conversation with Munch. A joke, he'd called it afterwards, in which he proposed she sit for Salome, and that he could be the severed head. She'd been so angry with him, scolding him through tears she was trying to hold back, saying it was crude, this comparison of any Jewish woman to Salome the wicked, the sensuous devourer of men.

Perhaps this is his apology.

"He did a nice sketch of the two of us," she says, feeling she ought to defend her peculiar friend.

"It wasn't too bad of you; I, however, am nothing but shivering scribbles. But then he never has cared for me."

"That's not true," Eva scolds.

"Yes it is, and I don't blame him; I don't like him either. We're competition for each other."

A lump rises in Eva's throat at this, and she looks away, down at her tea, anywhere but at Bella, unable to bear the implication.

When the silence is hurting her, she looks up at Bella, who is smiling generously back at her.

Bella crosses the room between them, wraps an arm around her waist and kisses her cheek.

"Do you like the picture?" she asks.

Eva leans her bony back into Bella's comforting warmth. "I do," she says.

"Good," Bella says, and kisses her again. "Then I shall like it too. Did you say he's coming to the concert tonight?"

Eva is startled away from her contemplation of the picture and looks at the clock.

"Heavens! Of course. Yes, yes he did say that. We should be getting ready." She starts away from Bella, sees Emiliani lying face down on the chaise-lounge, and sets him upright in the corner with a pang of guilt.

"Soon," Bella says gently. "No hurry." She has crossed the room and poured herself another cup of tea, which she drinks standing. "We have a few hours yet."

"Yes," Eva says faintly. "I suppose."

The day suddenly feels vast and uncertain around her, like a great whirling tempest she cannot control. She does not want to fall over, does not want to cry, does not want to confess the horror that is speeding up inside her. "Can we play something first?" she asks.

Bella nods, swigging back tea from fine china. "Indeed. What would you like to play?"

She and her tea cup are at the piano as Eva puts herself into motion, collecting Emiliani. "Could we play The Swan? Saint-Saens', not Greig's."

Bella nods. "I'd rather not Grieg. Yes, let's do Saint-Saens. That would be nice."

With no need for sheet music, they come together, and Bella begins the soft rippling of the piano, and Eva joins in with the gentle melody on her violin.

In their Berlin apartment, the two musicians play for no one but themselves.

An audience settling into their seats is not unlike an orchestra tuning up. Eva loves it. There are voices high and low, booming and muted: the hellos that reach from box to box are piccolo flutters, while the low cry of surprise as someone takes a thoughtless step backwards onto an self-important gentleman's shoe is a tuba expressing its blast. Each person is strung differently, some wound tight with excitement, some low and loose with boredom of being dragged to yet another concert. There is the familiar—they all know the part they are to play in the evening—mixed with the thrill of the unknown. Who will be there? Will young Johannes see the gentleman of whom he has been dreaming? Will the music inspire theories about art in Lotte that will exhaust her mother for the coming weeks? Will tante Hilde ask loudly, mid-performance, what music is being played, and cause her relatives to shrivel in their seats in embarrassment? Will ten year old Matilde look upon the beautiful Jewish lady playing the violin and soar with a joy she does not fully comprehend, but will lead her to beg for eine geige for her Christmas present?

The theatre is a place of habit and possibility.

While Bella takes the well-wishes of the theatre manager, the notices from the stagehands of five minutes until curtain up, the last-minute news of who has been spotted in the audience— while Bella of the sun takes all of this—Eva of the moon stands still as stone.

She tries to see herself as Munch has portrayed her, to muster the beauty of his art into her living being. Great, awful weight it is. The curtain severs her from the light of the world, wrapping her in a contained quiet that is adjacent to the great roar of chatter out in the auditorium but not part of it.

The world out there vibrates; hundreds of people, all buzzing with their thoughts and their lives, and she alone is here, cold and silent.

If only she could be like a picture of herself—still and complete, unable to make any mistakes.

A thing to be looked upon and contemplated.

Finished.

"Eva?"

The smooth warmth of Bella's palm lifts Eva's lifeless, bony fingers.

"Eva? Are you alright?"

Eva swallows, and looks up into Bella's lovely, round face; there is mild concern there, but reassurance too. The gold of her hair has a soft radiance in the half-light that creeps into backstage shadow.

Eva nods stiffly, her skull feeling impossibly heavy on her scrawny neck. "I don't want to do this."

"You never want to do this," says Bella's low resonance. "And yet you are always overjoyed to have done it. You will play and you will play beautifully, and those lucky people out there will have tears in their eyes at your incredible skill, and I will be beside you always, loving you."

Bella lightly brushes at the curls of Eva's dark hair, lifting them and shifting them back off her face. In that light movement, Eva feels a lightness in herself, a flexibility, and the sensation of Bella's breath on her cheek seems to be a spell of life, breathing blood and energy back into her.

Eva lets herself soften, folding her head into Bella's neck. She lifts Emiliani so he will not discomfort Bella, and will not be hurt himself, and allows him to nestle between them.

Beyond the thick curtain the audience has quieted in expectation, and a nod from a stagehand informs them it is time. He rushes off, and they are alone for two seconds. Eva takes Bella's face in her free hand and kisses her deeply before breaking away, breath short and bright-eyed.

Eva Muddoci and Bella Edwards walk onto the stage, the curtain rising before them, the audience turning its attention to applause. Like water splashing, each staccato clap contributes to a roaring waterfall of noise, from which wild whoops from faceless men fly out into the air to celebrate the players.

Bella is perfectly beside her; in a unison they have never needed to rehearse, they bow. Eva lifts the violin to her chin, and Bella sits at the piano. Hush falls. It is not the empty silence of despair but a fuzzy silence, a susurrus just below the hearing threshold of three hundred breathing bodies, bottoms shuffling in seats, fabrics pinched and pulled as wearers settle in. And Eva holds them all in her hand.

She lays the bow to the string, and Emiliani, gleaming in the gaslight, shines at her. He feels light, pliant, awaiting her.

We are magnificent, he whispers, and she smiles.

She can feel Bella's attention entirely a part of her, as if their minds inhabited the same metaphysical space outside their bodies, their drifting auras listening to one another.

In one gesture, Eva draws the bow long across the string, sounding the first longing note, then sliding down four more in a single fluid cry; a pause; Bella answers with a low, serious counterpoint, reassuring and encouraging; Eva and Emiliani leap into a fine, rich birdsong the celebrates the glimpse of sun beneath a bank of storm cloud.

The vibrations of the piano surround her and move through her. She closes her eyes to better feel the music, and holds Emiliani back, quietening their notes for Bella; the soft sustained notes draw out a melody that appreciates the rain and understands the storm.

This is their sonata. Later they will each perform solos by great men, but this is the conversation Bella has written just for them, and it is staggeringly, wonderfully true: they each have their moment to speak, they each reply, and they come together in an agreement that holds and respects difference.

Edvard Munch sitting in the audience is entirely forgotten, as is the great stone testament to his adoration of the beautiful violinist.

Eva has no thought of being the object of someone else's art. She is enthralled in life and creation and communion.

About the Author

DR. EZRA HARKER SHAW is a non-binary writer, academic, and award-winning author with a doctorate in Creative Writing. Born in Scotland and now based in London, they have published seven books across poetry and prose, with work appearing in journals, anthologies, and essay collections. A celebrated performance poet and playwright, Harker Shaw has been nominated for the Outspoken Prize for Poetry and serves as literary editor of *Selkie Songs*. Their teaching, editorial work, and doctoral research—including the award-winning novel *The Aziola's Cry*, inspired by Percy Bysshe and Mary Shelley—reflect a passion for the strange, the beautiful, and the bold.

The Blood of Englishmen

Cecil Beckett

25 June 1917

I AM AN EAGLE. I soar fifteen thousand feet high in the clouds and wait for prey beneath. I hunt not rabbits nor squirrels but the blood of Englishmen. My name is Manfred Albrecht Freiherr von Richthofen, and I am the Red Baron.

I wipe frozen breath from the windscreen with the back of my glove. I look down over the side of my Albatros D.III, and a hole has opened in the clouds, a gaping space that plunges straight down for over seven thousand feet with swirling walls of azure-blue mist. And at the bottom of this vast pit, I spy the quarry, a group of R.E.8s bumbling along like bees swollen with pollen.

I waggle my wings, for I hunt not alone but in a pack of brilliantly painted planes: the Jagdgeschwader, the Richthofen Flying Circus. Then I raise my hand to begin the dive, and the dazzle of blue, green, yellow, orange, and purple shapes into a perfect V formation behind my red wingtips. Down, down, down, and the wind howls between struts and wires, but our descent is measured, for the Albatros has a single-sparred lower wing that can tear from the fuselage in an undisciplined dive. The Red Baron is never reckless.

We are upon them before they see us. I swing onto the tail of the hindmost R.E. 8 and, with a burst of bullets, rip open the center of the machine and send the rear gunner straight to hell.

The pilot looks around, the fear in his eyes far too late as the plane bursts into flames. By now, the other R.E.8s realize we are amongst them, and the sky becomes a whirlpool of fighting machines. The Englishmen do not lack courage but are no match for the blaze of color surrounding them, and their doomed machines spin downwards in endless spirals of black smoke. Two of the English planes collide in a ball of fire. A stricken R.E.8 hurtles earthwards, dead Englishman slumped across the cockpit, and I have to maneuver out of the way. I fling the stick right over to the left, then hard back to the right, kick the right rudder simultaneously, and the Albatros swings up in a quick barrel roll, and I avoid disaster by less than a yard.

In the evening, I commission another silver goblet from Berlin. When it arrives, I will fill it with pear schnapps and toast the latest damned fool Englishman who thought they could fly in the same sky as the Red Baron. It will be my fifty-seventh silver cup.

6 July 1917

The day begins well enough. I am leading a squadron of eight above Wervik when we see six F.E.2s. We attack. Below me in his plum purple Albatros flies my comrade Oberleutnant Kurt Wolfe, and when I hear the hammering of a German machine gun, I know he has engaged in combat. Then the English plane in front of me turns and accepts the fight. The enemy's observer opens fire. I let the fool waste lead, for he is at least 300 yards away, and at that distance, even the best marksmanship is useless. Now, the plane is nearing me, and I swing the Albatros around and try to get behind my foe so I can riddle it with bullets. But a blow strikes me in the head. The pain is searing and absolute. I wipe a glove across my face, and it comes away covered in blood. My vision blurs and, for an awful moment, fades completely. I struggle to make my hands work. They are weak and seem not to belong to me. Then the damned F.E.2 is on my tail, and I throw my Albatros into a spin, somehow manage to come out, spin again, pull out once more, then push the stick forward and zigzag down toward the ground.

7 July – 4 September 1917

The doctor at the field hospital stares at me with somber, dark eyes. He is very short, and pimples cover both his cheeks. "You suffered a grave injury, Freiherr von Richthofen. Only by God's grace did you land your plane before you lost consciousness. A miracle."

"I am the Red Baron."

"Indeed, sir. But the bullet fractured the Red Baron's skull, and he has a cerebral hemorrhage. I have removed several bone splinters, but deeper ones remain in the frontal lobe that require neurosurgery. We need to transfer you to Cologne."

"I will stay here, thank you, doctor. I must get back to my Jagdgeschwader as soon as possible."

"I must insist."

He is an obstinate fellow, this little doctor. But I am the Red Baron, and I remain at the field hospital, and a neurosurgeon visits and anaesthetizes me and extracts pieces of bone from my brain. It is a difficult time. I have unrelenting headaches, lack appetite, suffer nausea and dizzy spells, insomnia, and a persisting weakness of grip in my left hand.

The doctor comes every morning, shines his torch into my pupils, and checks my reflexes with his hammer.

"Any symptoms, sir?"

"Feeling good, thank you, doctor. Bit of a headache."

The doctor looks at me sadly.

'Freiherr von Richthofen, if you are ever to recover fully, it will take many months, perhaps years. The damage from not only the physical brain injury but also the psychological toll is immeasurable. You need a long period of convalescence far away from the front."

"Doctor, every wretched fellow in the trenches must do his duty, and so will I."

I spend twenty days in the field hospital. I return to the skies on the twenty-first against the little doctor's orders. I have a hollow the size of a golf ball in my left temple, but I manage to fit my flying helmet over the bandages. On my first sortie, I shoot down a French Nieuport 23 over Polygon Wood. I accrue another three kills in the next two weeks, but when they tell me there is no silver left in Germany for my sixty-first goblet and will have to mold it from something else, I tell them not to bother.

I fear I am losing my passion for the hunt. I have a strange new depression and melancholy after each air combat.

5 September – 23 October 1917

I help myself to another schnapps in the officer's mess. Kurt Wolfe comes in and tells me there is a Generalleutnant to see me. He leads me next door to where the general sits in front of the fire with a few of the other officers: Edy Lulbert, Wilhelm Reinhard, and Hermann Goring.

"Good evening, General," I say, saluting.

"At ease, von Richthofen."

The general coughs and gets straight to the point. The German High Command doesn't want to risk the Red Baron being shot out of the skies, and they want me to take an extended period of leave.

"It would be bad for the country's morale if we lost you, my boy."

"I'll be the one doing the shooting down, sir. I got another only yesterday." I raise my glass. "A Sopwith Pup with a schoolboy pilot."

"I'm sorry, von Richthofen. But the stakes are too high. The English have promised a Victoria Cross to any man who shoots you down. We will not allow them to succeed. And your friends here have voiced some concerns since your accident."

Kurt's face flushes red, and Edy and Wilhelm stare into the fire, and I know at once who has been talking.

"What the devil have you said, Goring?"

"All the chaps have noticed. You are not yourself, Manfred." Goring's face looks like an overblown balloon. "You take far too many risks now. You fly too low through artillery fire. You do not know when to give up a chase. You have become rash, Manfred. And the drinking—you were always a temperate type, but now you fly drunk as an Englishman."

"That's a hell of a thing to say." I throw the empty glass into the fireplace.

My mother has our cook prepare the lung hash again. She knows it is my favorite, but I achieve only half a dozen mouthfuls.

"You need to strengthen yourself, Manfred. You are as thin as a rake."

"Goodnight, Mother." I take the bottle of wine up to my room.

The headaches persist, worse even, and I have a constant sickness in my stomach. I cannot sleep. The wine helps only so much, and I lie in a kind of purgatory between exhausted wakefulness and perfidious slumber. I have waking dreams of the wings snapping off my Albatros and the tanks exploding in flames, and I jolt upright in bed with my heart pounding, my hands shaking, and a taste of acid in my throat.

"You need some sunlight, Manfred."

My mother arranges for a young woman from church to walk with me. "You need someone to take your mind off this terrible war," my mother says. "Irmgard is so excited to see you again, Manfred."

No doubt, the poor girl is shocked to see what a broken-down, miserable wreck the Red Baron has become, but Irmgard is a beautiful, gentle, hopeful soul who takes my hand as we watch the ducks dive for frogs in the pond.

At dinner, I tell my mother I never want to see Irmgard again.

And then, one night, Percival arrives. He sits on the feather duvet at the end of my bed. He is a handsome fellow with curly blonde hair, cheerful blue eyes, and a bullet hole through his forehead.

"Who the hell are you?"

"Delighted to meet you too, old chap." He extends his hand, and I see the flesh on his right arm has burned down to the bone. "I'm Percival Murray. I copped a packet from you over France last February."

Winter 1917-1918

The war goes less well for Germany. We are losing superiority in the air, and the German High Command reconsiders its position on the Red Baron and hurries me back to the front. I am greatly relieved, for I fear I am going mad, and every day with my mother seemed only to hasten the madness.

The officers line up in the mess to shake my hand, even Goring. Wolfe is no longer with us. Edy Lulbert takes me outside and shows me my resplendent red Fokker DR-1.

"The latest triumph of German engineering," Edy says. "A triplane with exceptional maneuverability. It's good to have you back, Manfred."

"Kite's wasted on you, old chap," Percival says. "You'll wrap it around a tree."

The little doctor lost both his arms to an artillery shell whilst attending a patient at the lines and has been replaced by an older one who likes a drink and laughs all the time.

"Anything you need, Freiherr von Richthofen, anything at all. Just ask."

He prescribes a mixture of phenobarbital and chloral hydrate as a sleeping draught. "You'll sleep like the fairies."

I tell him about the headaches, and he laughs and assures me relief is at hand.

"You should have listened to your mother," Percival says. "You're a basket case. Completely barking mad. You're not fit to fly."

"At least I haven't got a bullet hole in my head."

"Well, that's not entirely true now, is it, Manfred?"

"Who are you talking to, sir?" asks my valet, handing me a steaming mug of coffee.

"Nobody. Bring me my flying jacket. And put a spot more rum in this coffee."

We level out at twelve thousand feet. The morphine the new doctor injected in my thigh this morning has resolved my headache, and I feel the most tremendous sense of elation and joy to be back in the air.

Percival is sitting on the nose of my plane, facing me, his back just behind the propeller, blonde curls blowing in the breeze. I kick the right rudder and jerk the stick back in an attempt to dislodge him. I must say the Fokker handles very well, and although the sudden movement provokes a certain dizziness and ringing in my left ear, I feel remarkably well.

Then I notice that Reinhard, who was flying at my right wingtip, appears to have fallen away in a spin. The other planes have broken formation and dropped far behind.

"You're a bloody menace in the sky," Percival says.

"I am the Red Baron." I have detected a small group of the new English S.E.5s flying back toward the lines, and the thrill of the hunt pumps through my veins once more.

"You can't catch them," Percival says. "They're not your usual cold meat."

I waggle my wings and raise my hand. Down, down, down, and the chill winter wind blasts against my face, and then the Fokker bounces through a patch of low cloud and bursts out the other side. I scan the skies, but the S.E.5s have disappeared. There is no sign of the rest of my Jagdgeschwader.

"You've lost them, old chap."

All around me, balls of white and black smoke explode, and I realize I am flying low, perhaps only three or four hundred feet, and I am over the enemy side of the lines, riding on a sea of anti-aircraft fire. Frustrated that I have not been able to get an S.E.5, I swing the Fokker around and strafe the Englishmen in the trenches below, up and down, up and down, until my guns are empty, watch the men dive for cover like startled ants.

"You're no sportsman," Percival says. "You're just a bloody butcher."

Goring corners me in the mess and grabs me around the throat.

"You're a disgrace to yourself and the Jagdgeschwader. You nearly killed Reinhard this morning. I refuse to fly with you ever again."

"If you had any balls, you'd punch the fat fuck in the face," Percival says.

But the doctor has given me my evening shot of morphine, and I just smile at Goring and disentangle myself from his spittle. I light a cigarette and choose a bottle to take to my room. I will drink the schnapps, take the pills the doctor has left me, and get a good night's sleep, and tomorrow, the Red Baron will be ready once more to hunt Englishmen.

Manfred Von Richthofen died on 22 April 1918. He was killed by a single bullet through the heart from an anti-aircraft gun while he was flying at a very low altitude over Morlancourt Ridge near the Somme River. He was 25 years old.

About the Author

CECIL BECKETT was born and raised in rural New Zealand. He enjoys writing short fiction about the past and the present. His short stories placed second in both the 2020 and 2021 Victoria Odyssey House Short Story Competition. He lives in Auckland with his wife and their cat.

No Shelter

Nicole M. Babb

THE WORLD IS CHANGING, and Cliff Burke hasn't yet decided if that's a good thing. People are afraid, and that can be useful, sure. But they also seem to have more fight in them. Especially the women.

Cliff whistles as he pulls his A55 Cambridge into the lot of Eagle Pencil Company at 8:45 a.m. His appointment isn't until ten, but he likes to be early. It gives him time to look around, make small talk. It doesn't hurt with sales, either.

He slips on the cheap wedding band he'd picked up a couple years back. Stepping from the car, he checks his reflection in the glossy black exterior. He looks sharp in the company uniform: clean-shaven, white shirt, black tie, dark gray suit. All part of the brand. No slovenly salesmen here. IBM is a well-oiled machine, from top to bottom. He grins at himself, winks.

He retrieves a heavy case from the backseat and heads inside, whistling softly. In the second-floor offices, he approaches a young secretary sitting in the center of the room. She looks up through long, dark lashes. No ring, he notes, as he smooths his tie, prominently displaying his own band.

"You're a sight for sore eyes," he says, "but don't tell my wife." There is no wife. The woman blushes. "I'm here for Mr. Berol. We have an appointment at nine."

She consults a daybook. "Mr. Burke? I have you down for ten."

"Ten? Gosh." He puts his hand to his head. "You know how it is, new baby, no one's sleeping at home—I must've gotten mixed up. I can wait in the car." No baby, either.

"Don't be silly. You'll wait right here."

"Only if you're sure."

"I'm sure. Coffee?"

"No, I'm fine. Really, you're the one I should be talking to." He taps the case.

"New typewriter?"

"Factory-fresh. This here's been a big hit. You're going to love it. How about I give you a little look-see now? Before Mr. Berol gets in. Then, when he comes, you can help me sell him on it." He winks.

"Sure. If you think I can help."

"I just bet you can." He pops the lid to reveal a beige typewriter with blue keys, checks her nameplate. "Nancy, meet the Selectric. The hottest model on the market. Look at this." He holds up a silver ball. "No more letters on a stick. You can change this one piece and get a completely different typeface."

"Isn't that something." She takes the type ball, examining it.

Now's his chance. "If the Russians don't blow us all to high heaven," he says.

"You don't think they will, do you?" Concern creases her forehead.

"I don't know what those guys are capable of. You heard what President Kennedy said a few weeks back—a fallout shelter for every American. And fast, too."

"I heard, but who can afford that?"

"You can go stay with your parents, though, can't you? If you had to?"

"My family's back in Iowa."

"Oh, I see. Well, we're some of the lucky ones. I know that. We've got a real top-of-the-line model. For bombs and fallout, both." This part was true.

This is the way he does it. Dribbles out information.
I have a wife.
I am safe.
A baby.
I'm safe.
A shelter.
Safe.

"Say—no, never mind. You wouldn't be interested."

Her eyes are very interested. "What's that?"

"My secretary just quit—got married a couple weeks back. I could get you a job. You could stay with us. We've got a suite over our garage you could have. Just until you can get your own place. It's not all that glamourous—for a girl like you—but you'd have a guaranteed spot in our shelter, too, if it comes to that."

"You'd have room?"

"It's for a family of four. We're only three."

"What would your wife think?"

"She'd love it. Having someone around to talk to, help with the baby. My last secretary lived over the garage. They got on like a house on fire."

"I hope you're not sweet-talking Nancy," says a deep voice behind Cliff.

He turns. "Mr. Berol? Cliff Burke." He extends a hand, and the man shakes it firmly.

"And what are you here to sell me? Not this machine." Mr. Berol eyes the Selectric.

"This machine, exactly, sir. I was just giving Nancy a preview."

"Tell me, what's so wrong with pencils? Writing things? It's like you don't even see these contraptions are going to put me out of business." Mr. Berol strides to his office, Cliff trailing behind.

"No, sir. The world will always need pencils. This just helps with efficiency. Think of the pencils you can sell with typed order forms! You'll double your business."

Three sales and $1,185 later, Cliff stops at Nancy's desk on his way out, slipping her his card. "Think about what I said.

Food, water, a safe place to sleep. You could survive at least a year down in that shelter. Apartment's not bad, either. Call if you're interested, you can come see the place for yourself."

Cliff comes out of the shelter whistling, stopping short when he sees the woman at his front stoop, dressed in a police uniform. She's peering through the window at the side of the door.

"Can I help you?" he asks, locking the shelter.

The woman whirls, caught red-handed. "I was knocking. I'm looking for Cliff Burke."

"That'd be me. What can I do you for?"

"Mary Goodwin with NYPD. I'd like to ask you a few questions." She pulls three slips of paper from her pocket and holds them out to him.

"A police lady, huh? You girls are getting into everything nowadays. And all the way up from New York City to see me." He gives her his signature grin.

She doesn't smile back. "We sure are everywhere now, over 200 of us policewomen if you believe it." She looks behind him, examining the domed structure protruding from the earth.

He steps forward to take the papers from her. Photographs.

"Do you know any of these women, Mr. Burke?"

He did. "Can't say I do."

"You sure?"

"What's this about?"

"Nancy Booker, Patricia Howard, and Joanne Russell. All missing."

"From New York City?"

"No, we're working with other departments. Miss Howard is from New York City. The others are from Danbury and New Haven."

"How would I know anything about these women, Miss Goodwin?"

"Officer Goodwin. The women have a few things in common. They were all secretaries."

"Lots of women are secretaries."

"They all used Selectric typewriters."

"Almost every secretary in the country is using a Selectric right now. They're revolutionary."

"And you were the salesman for all three. Your territory's the Northeast, right?"

He examines the photos again, holds up Nancy's grinning face. "I think I might have met her once. The other two, I can't recall."

"Do you have an apartment above your garage?"

"I do. Why, you looking for a room? I never use it."

"Joanne Russell told her sister she was coming up here. Something about a job at IBM. Said she was going to rent a room from you. That it came with a spot in your shelter." She nods to the white concrete dome.

"Half the town has a garage apartment. And a shelter."

"What happened to your neck?"

He rubs the deep scratch just under his chin. Nancy happened. All that fight. "Yardwork. Branch caught me."

Her eyes flicker back to the bunker. "That's some shelter you've got there. Must've cost a pretty penny."

"It did. The company fronted the money for employees to get shelters. Figured I might as well get a blue-ribbon model. It's a Fam-Shel. Nothing more important than safety."

"Mmm. Mind if I take a look?"

They descend in silence, save for the click of their shoes on metal steps and the hum of the overhead lights. At the bottom of the stairs is a mid-size room with two sets of narrow bunk beds.

"Quiet down here," she says.

"With the door closed, it's soundproof." His voice has lost its chipper tone.

A door in the far-right corner opens to a small room; brown cardboard canisters marked "Sanitation Supplies" are visible from the main room. To the left, a room with no door is shrouded in black.

"What's this?" Officer Goodwin asks, pulling a flashlight

from her belt. She sweeps the light around the dark room.

"This is what'll keep me alive. Water, food, medicine. Everything I need."

Black steel barrels labeled "Drinking Water" line one wall, along with several nearly identical but unmarked barrels. She approaches the plain barrels and grasps the lip of the lid. "And these?"

Cliff takes a sudden step forward. "Don't. Extra water. Can't break the seal."

"Lot of water." Officer Goodwin hesitates for a long moment, eyes on Cliff.

His own eyes sparkle with excitement. He reaches a hand toward her. Will he have to? Not ideal. Police officer is likely to put up a fuss. He'll come out with more than a scratch, if he comes out at all.

She swallows hard, then relents. "Thanks for your time, Mr. Burke. I'll see myself out. Call if you think of anything." She ascends the steps alone, leaving Cliff standing in the storage closet, heart pounding.

Not so much fight, after all.

Cliff waits weeks before he so much as looks at another woman, but when he sees Peggy Leonard, he knows he's got to have her. She has shiny black hair and full lips. Most importantly, she's not wearing nylons. Her smooth, bare legs disappear into a skirt just above the knee.

He's back in Danbury, where he found Nancy Booker. A different company, but still, it's a risk. He glances around, sure Officer Goodwin's watching him.

Once he's certain the only eyes on him are Peggy's, Cliff starts his routine. He smooths his tie with his left hand, flashing his fake ring. "I'm here for Mr. Carlisle. We have an appointment at nine."

Peggy plays her part perfectly. "Mr. Burke? I have you down for ten."

He slaps his forehead. "Oh gosh. I haven't been sleeping

too well, with the new baby, you know. I can wait out in the car."

"Of course not. Coffee?"

On his way out, he drops her his card. "Think about it. If you're interested, it's yours. A room for now and for World War III."

Peggy takes a cab from the train station. Cliff's waiting out front, whistling when she steps into the drive holding a hard-sided yellow suitcase in one hand, hat box in the other.

He waits for the green and white monstrosity to leave. He likes to shuffle them straight down to the shelter. It gets complicated, bringing them inside. But the car idles, oblivious to the jam it's putting him in.

"Let me show you to your room." He reaches for her suitcase, noting his own bare ring finger too late. If she notices, she doesn't say anything, but her green eyes shimmer with curiosity and she holds his gaze for a moment, her mouth turned up in a slight smile.

Cliff leads her through the detached garage, up a staircase, and into a small one-room apartment. The walls are a dingy yellow. Cobwebs fill the corner and the curtains are lined with dust. A cockroach scrabbles across the kitchenette counter.

"Sorry. My wife's been busy with the baby, we didn't have time to get everything ready. I'll help you clean this place up."

Peggy nods. "Where is she?"

"Who?"

"Your wife, and the baby. I'd love to meet them. If I'm going to be living here." She adds the last part as if an afterthought.

"Oh, right. She took the baby to her mother's. They'll be back around dinner. You can meet them then." He walks to the grime-caked window. The cab's finally gone.

There's a silent pause. Peggy sets her things on the floor, not commenting on the lack of furniture.

"Why don't I show you the pièce de resistance?" he asks.

"Oh, that's alright. I think I'll just tidy up in here and come down when your wife gets home."

"No, no, come on. You've got to see it. It's why you're here, isn't it?" He touches her waist. She doesn't remove his hand as he leads her back through the garage to the white dome and unlocks the door, gesturing for her to enter.

She peers inside. "Oh, it's deeper than I imagined. You go ahead of me so you can catch me if I trip." She gives his arm a squeeze and leans into him. His heart races. She won't be a problem. Not like that awful Nancy.

"Pull that door closed, will you?" he asks, looking at her over his shoulder. He watches to make sure it's secure before continuing down the steps. "So, what do you think?"

She leans forward so her words tickle his ear. "You want to know what I think?"

Her hands press against his shoulder blades.

"I think you don't have a wife."

A push.

"Or a baby."

The reinforced concrete floor of the bunker is the last goddamn thing Cliff Burke sees.

It doesn't take Officer Goodwin long to show up at Cliff's once Peggy Leonard is reported missing. She knocks on the door, again peering through the sidelight. This time, she's ready for him. She holds a photo in one hand. The other rests on her sidearm.

The door opens. Officer Goodwin looks from the photo to the woman standing before her. "Peggy? Peggy Leonard?"

"Yes, that's me. Can I help you?"

"I'm looking for you. Your boss said you haven't shown up to work all week."

"Well, I'm right here," Peggy says with a wide smile.

"And the man who lives here? Mr. Burke. He around?"

"He's down in the shelter. Let's go see." Peggy crosses the yard to the bunker. She pulls a key from her pocket and unlocks the door.

Officer Goodwin's skin prickles, though she can't quite put

her finger on why. Had she been wrong about Cliff Burke? Peggy reaches her arm in and flips on the overhead lights. "Go on down, officer. I'll wait."

Officer Goodwin steps to the door, greeted only by the hum of lights. She waits for Cliff to call out, run up the steps.

Nothing.

She turns back to Peggy, who's watching her with an intensity that makes her skin crawl. "You know what, I don't want to bother him. I came looking for you. You're safe. My job here's done."

Peggy gives a slow nod, not breaking eye contact. "Be safe out there, officer."

"You too, Peggy. You too."

In her rearview mirror, Officer Goodwin watches as Peggy turns off the lights and locks the shelter door. World War III or not, Cliff Burke won't ever be leaving that shelter. And that's just fine with her.

About the Author

NICOLE BABB is a recovering litigator who is using her exit from the world of facts to write stories that exist somewhere between the real and not-real. Her favorite stories include larger-than-life characters and an extra helping of snark. She's a lifelong New Orleanian, and when she's not writing enjoys good wine, the occasional bad wine, yoga, and board games. Her work has appeared in *Does It Have Pockets* and *Foofaraw*, and in 2024, she was awarded the Scribes Prize for Microfiction. Find her at nicolebabb.com.

The Presbyterian Settee

Rob Hardy

1982

THE SUMMER BEFORE MY SENIOR YEAR in high school, a series of financial setbacks forced my parents to sell our home and move forty miles from the village where I had grown up to another village on the other side of Cayuga Lake. I stayed behind in a rented room at the edge of the school district, seven miles from the high school. For the first time in my life I had to ride the school bus, stopping and starting down dirt roads between cornfields for more than an hour morning and afternoon. Over the summer I had become a ghost. On weekdays I haunted the halls of the high school. On weekends, I vanished across the lake. Life in the village went on without me.

Sometimes I stayed after school and the bus left without me, and I found myself homeless in my hometown. The pastor of the Presbyterian Church had given me a key to the chapel, the smaller building next to the church that housed the fellowship hall, kitchen, Sunday School rooms, and the pastor's office. There were usually leftovers from coffee hours or potlucks in the refrigerator so I could feed myself. In the pastor's office there was a small settee where I could sleep. I knew the settee was old—nineteenth-century old—and had once stood in the back of the sanctuary.

I had sat on that settee four years earlier during confirmation classes. The only other confirmand was a girl. We sat so uncomfortably close that our legs sometimes touched, which made it difficult to keep my attention on grace and predestination. But it felt at the time like I was entering a new period of belonging, like I was being written into a bigger story.

Four years later, there I was on that small sofa, alone in the dark, curled into the fetal position like a child returned to the womb and awaiting a second birth.

I don't know if I felt the presence of God in the dark, but I did feel the presence of the past, both my own past and the past that stretched back beyond me, but to which I had also once belonged by belonging to the village. I seemed to stir the past up with my passing, to disturb it with my brief turbulence. But in stillness of the chapel at night, I wasn't afraid of ghosts. I was one of them.

I knew the settee had a story, and now I was part of the story. A continuation.

1828

In 1828, a body washed up on the shore of Lake Ontario. The body was bloated and fish-eaten and ghastly, but from a small scar still visible about the right eyebrow it was allegedly identified as the body of William Morgan, who had gone missing two years earlier after making a deal with a printer in Batavia to publish a book exposing the secrets of the Freemasons.

Depending on who you talk to around here, this Morgan was either a scoundrel and a liar or the victim of a conspiracy to silence him. He passed himself off as Captain William Morgan, but there were those who doubted the stories of his distinguished service in the War of 1812. He also claimed to have advanced to the degree of Royal Arch Mason, but again there were doubts, and the doors of the Batavia lodge were shut against him.

On the other hand, it's a fact that someone attempted to set fire to the printer's office where Morgan's book was being printed. It's a fact that after announcing his intention to publish the book, Morgan was suddenly arrested for an unpaid debt, sent to debtors' prison, released on bail, arrested again, and released a second time on bail. And after he was released the second time, he disappeared without a trace. Two years later, a body washed up on the shore of Lake Ontario.

These were the facts as W. W. Phelps laid them out for me in the office of The Lake Light, the new Anti-Masonic newspaper in Trumansburg, New York.

You'll want to know about me, I suppose, since I'm the one telling this story. There's not much to tell. My name doesn't matter. I was sixteen and looking for work. Mr. Phelps's newspaper was a new business here in town, and I was figuring to get in on the ground floor as a printer's devil—a boy who sorts the type, cleans the press, sweeps the floor, brings the printer his cup of coffee, and thereby learns the art of printing.

"If anything about the Freemasons is as clear as day," Mr. Phelps said, "it's that they were behind the persecution, disappearance, and murder of Captain William Morgan."

He pounded the desk with the flat of his hand for emphasis and raised a small cloud of dust.

"Who are the most influential members of any community?" he asked. "The Freemasons. They control the majority of the public offices, but for the most part they operate in secret and in such a way as to be answerable to no one but themselves. Look at the men of the first rank in this town. Let us but name Lyman Strowbridge. Pass by his place of residence late at night and you will see a light burning in his window. Should you tarry long enough you might see a dozen other men issuing forth from his door. What do you suppose can be their purpose?"

"I suppose the study of Scripture?" I suggested.

Mr. Strowbridge was a prominent member of the First Presbyterian Church, where on Sunday mornings I could see the back of his bowed head from my family's pew in the aft of the sanctuary. The church had been caught up in the blaze of religious revivalism that had swept over western New York, and on Sunday mornings the pews were full of the elect warming their souls on the fire and brimstone from the pulpit.

"Nay, if they study aught it is their own interests," he said.

"I approached Rev. Carle with the facts as I have stated them to you, and attempted to impress upon him the urgency of rooting Masonry out of his congregation. But the man is a Mason himself! There you see the depths of the conspiracy. There you see how tenaciously Freemasonry has rooted itself in positions of influence in society. These Masons killed Captain Morgan, you can be sure of it. But they're too subtle and secretive to have the crime laid to their account, and so they must be prosecuted in the court of public opinion."

Mr. Phelps had a persuasive style, which I am doing my best to render just as I heard it from his own mouth. He also wrote poetry, as an example of which I give you the following stanza:

> It is a solemn grief and pleasure,
> To muse among the slumb'ring dead—
> A time of gloomy, holy leisure,
> As o'er silent tombs we tread.

Observe how two seemingly opposite propositions, grief and pleasure, can stand together in the same line without canceling each other out.

He paused to take a breath, then finally came around to the business at hand.

"I will make you an offer," he said. "I will employ you on a trial basis, provided you can render certain services to advance the interests of this newspaper. I have become too prominent in my position as editor of the Lake Light to maintain a close observation of the Masonic inner circle of this town with a view to exposing their secrets. I want you to insinuate yourself into the confidence of Mr. Strowbridge and report to me anything that might further the Anti-Masonic cause."

With a handshake, we sealed the agreement between us.

Like the line in Mr. Phelps's poem, which holds both grief and pleasure, Trumansburg's wide Main Street held both mud and dust, depending on the inclination of the weather. It likewise held both the Anti-Masonic Mr. Phelps and the Masonic Mr. Strowbridge, the latter of whom could be found at his harness shop, which stood side-by-side with the blacksmith shop of Mr. Creque—the two men together forming a partnership that keeps the farms between Cayuga and Seneca Lakes supplied with cast-iron plows and all their rigging.

The shop smelled of leather and iron, saddle soap and pine boards. I preferred its earthiness to the smell of newsprint. I reflected that if I followed my nose to a vocation, I would become a harness maker instead of a printer. I told Mr. Strowbridge I was looking for work. Finding that I knew nothing about plows, he set about to educate me.

"Naturally Mr. Creque, being a blacksmith, is the one to tell you about plows," Mr. Strowbridge said, "but I'll try my best to do justice to the subject. Your basic plow has three main parts. The share cuts the sod, the moldboard turns over the sod, and the landside keeps the plow running straight in the furrow. Now, the plows our fathers and grandfathers had back east had a wrought iron share and landside attached to a wooden moldboard. In your typical rocky soil, like here in New York and back there in New England, the moldboard was always being smashed to bits. Well, this gentleman over near Scipio, Mr. Jethro Wood, had the idea of casting all three parts in iron."

Mr. Strowbridge had plenty to say about cast-iron plows. It turned out that not only were cast-iron parts more durable, they were also interchangeable. If a part did break beyond repair, it could be replaced with an identical part cast from the same mold.

His enthusiasm for the subject of cast-iron plows seemed to me not unlike Mr. Phelps's enthusiasm for the subject of Masons. It was an age of enthusiasms—political, entrepreneurial, and religious. It was an age of beginnings, of men heading west to start over in a new place, of new towns and villages dotting the map and spreading like a cartographic pox. It was an age of enterprise, when each one of those tiny dots on the map dreamed itself bigger. Trumansburg was one of those tiny dots.

We walked over to the lot on Union Street where Mr. Creque was building a foundry that would make it possible for him to produce his own castings. As I stood there on the vacant lot, I had a kind of vision. There, where an older building had recently been torn down, a new foundry would be built. Eventually the foundry itself would be torn down and something else would be built in its place. And so, in the course of time, many different structures in succession would occupy the same site. The village itself, like Mr. Wood's cast iron plow, was constructed of replaceable parts.

At the time, all of the iron parts sold by Mr. Creque and Mr. Strowbridge were cast in Mr. Wood's shop and brought by wagon over from Poplar Ridge, thirty-five miles away on the far side of the lake. Mr. Strowbridge was leaving for Poplar Ridge in the morning, and engaged me to accompany him on the journey.

We left for Mr. Wood's at first light on Friday. The weather was settled and dry, the road was good, and we had every expectation of reaching our destination before nightfall. We took the stage road out of town, heading south to Ithaca, then up the other side of Cayuga Lake to Poplar Ridge. We rolled through a pleasant landscape of orchards and fields, stopping once or twice to talk to a farmer working his field behind a cast-iron plow.

"Mr. Wood holds the patent on the cast-iron parts I showed you back at the shop," Mr. Strowbridge told me, "and he retains no less a man than former President John Quincy Adams to represent his claims in court. But I can tell you this, that President Adams profits more from the cast-iron plow than Mr. Wood does."

I understood that Mr. Creque and Mr. Strowbridge weren't going to let a small thing like a patent stand in the way of making their own castings. The legal risk seemed slight compared to the potential for profit. With a few modifications, the Wood plow would become the Creque Iron Plow.

"Have you read Mr. Phelps's newspaper?" I asked.

"Phelps? That man just stirs up trouble so he can profit from it. It sells newspapers. There's no truth in anything he prints once you get past the date at the top of the front page. I might be persuaded the day is Friday, but beyond that I wouldn't credit anything else."

"You don't believe the Masons had anything to do with Captain Morgan's death?"

"There's a long list of things I don't believe. I don't believe the man was ever a captain. I don't believe the body they found in Lake Ontario was Morgan's. And, no, I don't believe Freemasons had anything to do with it. The whole thing's a ploy to gain votes for the Anti-Masonic Party. I hear Thurlow Weed said anybody that washes up on shore is a good enough Morgan until after the election."

I knew Thurlow Weed was the political boss who was turning the Anti-Masonic Party into the main opposition party in our part of New York State. According to Mr. Strowbridge, men like Weed and Phelps were opportunists. But it seemed to me that everyone was on the lookout for an opportunity. Here were Mr. Strowbridge and Mr. Creque, looking for an opportunity to cut out Mr. Wood and make their own plow castings. Everyone was just waiting for a body to wash up on shore.

A few miles north of Ithaca, before the sharp descent to the lake, we stopped to talk to a farmer who handed me an arrowhead he had just turned up with this plow. I wondered how it had come to be buried in a field. I turned the arrowhead over in my hand. Someone had fashioned it from flint and held it as I held it now. I felt somehow connected to the maker of that arrowhead, to some unknown person who had existed once in the world but existed now only in my imagination.

"I still find quite a few arrowheads," the farmer said. "And charred wood. I think there might have been an orchard here."

Just fifty years ago, this had been the land of the Iroquois, and General John Sullivan had been sent by General Washington to burn their fields and orchards in retaliation for their support of the British. The past was so close to the surface. The land held onto it.

We put up for the night in Poplar Ridge, and on Saturday

morning we went around to Mr. Wood's shop and loaded the plow castings into the wagon. The added weight of the castings slowed our return journey, forcing us to spend another night on the road before reaching Trumansburg. We stopped for the night at an inn the other side of Ithaca and got an early start the next morning. Mr. Strowbridge wanted to be back in time for church.

I can't say I got much out of the journey, other than the arrowhead in my pocket and the dollar Mr. Strowbridge gave me for helping him load and unload the wagon. There was nothing I could tell Mr. Phelps about the Masons. After spending two days with Mr. Strowbridge, I was inclined to accept his view that the whole Morgan business was a fabrication, either to sell newspapers or gain votes, or both. I had half a mind not to go back to Mr. Phelps on Monday morning now that I had earned an honest wage from Mr. Strowbridge.

"Tell me again," Mr. Phelps said.

He was unexpectedly aroused by my account of the uneventful journey I had made with Mr. Strowbridge. He took notes as I spoke and asked me to repeat certain details. There were things I held back from my account, such our brief conversation about Mr. Wood's patent, and I was careful to include only such things as reflected well on Mr. Strowbridge, such as the fact that he was eager to return home in time to attend the Sunday service. This spoke to his good character as a member of the church.

"To review," Mr. Phelps said, looking at his notes, "you left Trumansburg on Friday morning and arrived in Poplar Ridge on Friday evening. On Saturday morning you commenced the homeward journey, traveling as far as Davenport's tavern by nightfall. You resumed the journey early on Sunday morning, and arrived in Trumansburg in time for the service at the Presbyterian Church. Is everything correct as I have repeated it back to you?"

"Yes, sir."

"Splendid," he said.

He pulled open the top drawer of his desk and took out a half dollar, which he placed into my hand.

"I don't understand, sir," I said. "I told you everything that happened, and it's nothing."

"In this business, you develop an eye for the kernel of a story," he said. "You think on everything you've told me, and see if you can't find the kernel."

It wasn't until I read the story in the next issue of the Lake Light that I recognized what Mr. Phelps had called the kernel of the story. The story Mr. Phelps wrote was about how Lyman Strowbridge, a noted Mason and prominent member of the First Presbyterian Church, had traveled for business on the morning of the Sabbath.

"It is to be hoped that the church will take appropriate action to address this clear breach of the Fourth Commandment, which enjoins upon the faithful the obligation to remember the Sabbath and keep it holy," Mr. Phelps had written.

It was a small item, but it was brought to the attention of the church elders, who promptly voted to expel Mr. Strowbridge from his pew. Without his pew, Mr. Strowbridge was effectively removed from the congregation.

I had also traveled on the Sabbath, but this went unmentioned. The sole purpose of the story was to discredit Mr. Strowbridge, and he was the only person named. For many days after the story appeared this weighed on my conscience. I did not return to the office of the Lake Light to pursue my ambition of becoming a printer's devil, nor did I return to Mr. Strowbridge's shop. I began to consider what other employment I might find suitable, perhaps in some other town. I found myself thinking about William Morgan, the man who disappeared. A man who made himself out of stories until nothing was left of him but a story. Maybe I would disappear into a story.

On Sunday morning, I loitered outside the church after my parents had gone in. A few other stragglers greeted me as they went inside. I could hear the voices of the congregation swell each time the door of the church was opened. I was thinking I might just stay there, on the outside, when a wagon pulled up on the street outside the church. The driver was Mr. Strowbridge.

"There you are!" he called down to me.

He jumped down from the seat and walked around to the back of the wagon.

"Where have you been keeping yourself? Why don't you come over and give me a hand."

In the back of the wagon was a small settee, upholstered in brown fabric, with scrolled armrests, just wide enough for two people.

"My new pew," he said.

I helped him unload the settee from the wagon and carry it into the church. The entire congregation turned to watch us as we set the sofa down against the wall at the back of the sanctuary and took our seats on Mr. Strowbridge's pew.

1882

Lyman Strowbridge died this past March. He was buried in Grove Cemetery, out by the woods south of town. His eulogists remembered his services to the village, the church, and the Masonic lodge. A passing reference was made to his settee.

In 1849, the Presbyterians demolished the old wooden church and replaced it with a new brick church in the Greek Revival style. After the new church was built, the elders put Mr. Strowbridge's settee back in its place at the back of the sanctuary. It's curious how these things happen.

I'm one of the few people still living who was there and can tell first-hand the story of that article of furniture. I may have added a few embellishments, but that's the way with stories. The past doesn't always stand still. Even the settee itself has been reupholstered, its threadbare brown fabric replaced with broad rose-colored stripes. A village is made of replaceable parts. I imagine someone in another century sitting there, imagining me in the past, the settee being the only thing that connects us. Its reality a bridge between two imaginations.

About the Author

ROB HARDY grew up in the Finger Lakes Region of New York, where his story is set; majored in History and Latin at Oberlin College; and served as the first Poet Laureate of Northfield, Minnesota. He has published fiction, poetry, and nonfiction, including two nonfiction pieces in Minnesota History.

The God of Sight

Morgan Want

HAGAR KNEW HER TIME with Abraham was coming to an end when she saw her mistress, Sarah, watching her at the feast for Isaac's weaning. Hagar had been laughing with the other women until she noticed her. In the years that she'd lived and traveled with Abraham's household, Hagar had come to know her mistress's moods the way some men knew the weather by the way of the winds, and suffering always followed Sarah's displeasure. And yet, Hagar was still surprised when, a few days later, Abraham came to her tent before sunrise, and told her to gather all the supplies she could carry, along with her son, Ishmael.

Abraham had two camels ready at the edge of his camp by the time she'd roused Ishmael. He stood alone, a thin silhouette against the shrinking dark, without any other servants, and yet someone had loaded the camels with extra water skins and supplies.

"Where are we going, Abba?" Ishmael asked, still blinking away sleep.

He frowned at the tents nestled together like sleeping sheep. There was no business Abraham would take a fifteen-year-old boy and his mother on alone, and even a sudden decampment would still come with at least a day's warning, so Hagar and the other women could pack while the men prepared the herds to move.

"Such a bright boy," Hagar thought. "And he was cursed with a fool for a mother."

She should have started making preparations after the feast, perhaps sooner. She knew better than anyone Sarah's capacity for spite; she should have known her mistress would no longer suffer Hagar's presence after Isaac was born. But Hagar never believed, until that moment, that Sarah could persuade him to send his first born away, even if he was the son of a lowly slave turned concubine.

"I cannot say," Abraham said. "You and your mother are to travel alone from here."

"Alone? But—without you?" sputtered Ishmael. "Why?"

Tears glistened in Abraham's dark eyes, like the dew upon the rocks. He looked at Hagar, but she kept her lips pressed together. She would not help him. He could break their son's heart alone.

"Sarah wishes it," Abraham said at last. "And it's the will of El that I do as she asks."

The will of El. What an excellent way to absolve himself of any guilt.

"I don't understand, Abba," Ishmael said.

"Nor do I, my son, but I trust El. And He has told me that you shall not perish when you leave here, but will grow to father a great nation, like your brother."

He cupped Ishmael's face in his hands. Tears ran down both their cheeks.

"You have no idea how much I wish I could go with you, to witness it," Abraham whispered. "Your mother will be by your side in my stead, and I trust her, more than anyone. She is a wise woman. See that you listen to her."

He looked up at Hagar from over the top of their son's head. His own hair was as white as the snow atop the mountains, and his face just as ancient. He was old when Hagar was given to him in Egypt, over a decade ago, but the look in his eyes was as uncertain as a child's. Hagar softened. She couldn't help it, she'd miss the old man.

One of the male servants came running from the tents. He was a faceless shadow against the ground, but Hagar recognized his voice when he spoke to Abraham.

"Master," he panted. "I come from Mistress Sarah. She asks—"

He stopped and swallowed, likely trying to catch his breath, but Hagar thought she saw him glance at her. It was hard to be certain in the dark.

"She asks that you not give any of your camels to the slave girl or her son."

"She... what?" Abraham exclaimed.

"And she—she also wants to remind you of your promise to do whatever she asks of you in this matter."

Hagar looked back at the tents, where Sarah was no doubt watching, waiting to see her reaction to this final slight. Well, Hagar would not give her the satisfaction. No matter what Sarah might call her, Hagar wasn't her slave any longer.

"Fine then," Hagar said, taking a water skin off one of the camels. "We won't take them then. I wouldn't want to cause a quarrel between you and your wife, after all."

Abraham flinched, but it did not give Hagar the pleasure she thought it would. He was still the father of her son, and no matter what might pass between Hagar and Sarah, that fact would never change. Ishmael would not see his parents part in anger.

"You need not worry about your son," she said. "As you said, I will care for him, no matter what."

"We will take care of each other, Mut," Ishmael said, addressing her with the Egyptian word for mother.

She turned away from Ishmael, on the pretense of taking another water skin off the camels, so she could blink away the tears pricking her eyes like hot needles. Ishmael was a man now, and had been considered so for years, yet he still looked like a boy. And it was hard for Hagar not to see him as one as well.

"Remember," Abraham said. " This is the will of El. All will be well. Shalom, my son."

"Shalom, Abba," Ishmael said, embracing his father.

A thin, blue blade of light unsheathed itself over the wilderness of Beersheba, and Hagar shivered at the sight of the unbroken desert. The shrubs that covered the hills were as dark and dry as the sand they grew from, and Hagar knew there were creatures living beneath them that she couldn't see. She was not looking forward to traveling on foot, but she also knew that if she did not start walking soon, Abraham and Ishmael might cling together forever.

"Come, Ishmael," she said. "Let's go."

"Where are you taking us, Mut?"

The sun was rising, glowering down at them like a bloodshot eye.

"Egypt," Hagar said. "We're going to Egypt."

She still remembered the way, even if it had been years since she'd crossed the desert with Abraham and his caravan. They just had to keep walking east, towards the sun, the eye of the sky god, Horus. Did his gaze extend beyond Egypt? And did he see her and Ishmael now, standing like two lonely pillars in the desert? Once, Hagar wouldn't have thought to ask such questions, but now, after all she'd seen and experienced over the last fifteen years, she wasn't certain what their answers would be. Horus never spared her a glance before. Not like...

Hagar's underarms already felt wet with sweat. Perhaps it was best not to contemplate the sun too much during their journey.

"Why do we not go to Beersheba, or one of the other cities near here?" Ishmael asked. "At least for now. I could find work, and—"

"No."

"But the journey to Egypt will be—"

"We can make it with what we have," Hagar said. "Please do not argue with me."

Ishmael tightened his jaw, but nodded. Hagar softened her voice.

"Please trust me in this. I've traveled this route before, and remember it well."

Hagar was also trying to remember the locations of every

spring and well along the way, particularly the ones away from the trade road that stretched across Canaan.

"You're afraid, aren't you, Mut?" Ishmael said.

Hagar hesitated, then nodded.

"There are many people who resent your father for his wealth. I do not think it's wise to make it known that we are no longer under his protection."

There were other dangers to consider as well: slave traders who would be eager to prey on a lone woman and her son. Or worse. Robbers who might abuse them both, and leave them dead or dying afterwards.

"But we are still under El Roi's protection," Ishmael said.

El Roi. The name Hagar gave to Abraham's God. Ishmael rarely used it himself, usually choosing to simply refer to Him as El, like his father. The gesture was enough to make Hagar nod in concession.

"Yes," she said, but Ishmael must have heard the uncertainty in her voice.

"You said He came to you the last time you tried to leave," Ishmael said. "Why would He protect you then, only to abandon you now?"

Yes, Hagar thought. Why?

El Roi had protected her once before, when she was pregnant and alone in the wilderness, driven away by Sarah's abuses. He'd told her not to be afraid to return to her mistress. To submit to her. Did He not know she would be cast away later? Or had He not cared?

Hagar looked at Ishmael. Of all the pain she'd endured in her life, she'd at least been spared the pain of being turned out by her own father.

"I don't know," she admitted. "I do not want to talk about these things any longer."

All this talk was doing nothing but making her mouth dry. She took a sip of water from one of their skins and held it in her mouth. Hot as the day would be, Hagar knew it would be preferable to the night, when the desert would become frigid, and it would be impossible to see any snakes or scorpions that might creep out from beneath the rocks. And then there were the larger animals, like the wolves and jackals that shared the visage of Egypt's death god, Anubis. They might leap out and surprise them in the dark.

Just thinking about it made Hagar's heartbeat quicken. Perhaps they should try to break a couple branches off a shrub, or one of the little pistachio trees that grew on the hills, so they would not be completely defenseless.

"Fine," Ishmael said. "Whatever you wish. May I have a drink then?"

Hagar handed him the water skin, and tried not to wince when he took a longer drink than she had.

He's lived in the desert all his life, she reminded herself. He knows it's important to conserve water.

It would be better, though, if they could keep their minds off their thirst as much as possible. Hagar licked her lips to moisten them before speaking.

"Let's talk of Egypt instead," she said. "You will need to know it well, if you are to live there."

"As I said, whatever you wish," Ishmael said.

Hagar ignored his sullen tone.

"Egypt is the land of the river," she said. "Every summer it breaks out of its banks to flood and water the earth. Its habits never change, and all who live by it can rely on it."

Most people in Egypt even believed the river was a god, but Hagar knew what Ishmael would say if she told him that: that El Roi was the only God. So she went on.

"My mother's house was on a little hill by the bank. She was a slave as well, but she was allowed her own house, in a little village, with other slaves. Real houses that never move, not like tents. Can you imagine, Ishmael? We will have our own house too, because no one who lives by the river ever has to wander, as the desert people do. Even the flies and mosquito hatchlings stay near its banks."

In fact, Hagar remembered one summer, when she was

a little girl, when they were so abundant, she was constantly scratching at little red bumps on her arms and legs. She would wake up with their tiny black legs tickling her lips like a kiss. Then she grew too sick to shoo them away. Her mother had to swat them away for her, while she prayed the prayer of protection for children. The one meant to ward off the demons who came in the night with backwards faces.

Hagar did not remember much from that time, but she did remember hearing her mother's voice intone that ancient prayer:

> *May she flow away—she who comes in the darkness,*
> *Who enters furtively*
> *With her nose behind her, her face turned*
> *Backward—*
> *Failing in that for which she came!*
> *Have you come to kiss this child?*
> *I will not let you kiss her! Have you come to harm her?*
> *I will not let you harm her!*
> *Have you come to take her away?*
> *I will not let you take her away from me!*

She remembered, also, seeing her mother's eyes hover over her. The most beautiful eyes Hagar had ever seen. Hagar had had few opportunities to look at her own reflection, but those who'd known them both told her they shared the same eyes. Not long after Hagar's opened again, clear of fever, her mother's eyes closed for good.

"The river is the source of life," Hagar finished.

"But El Roi was the one who blessed you," Ishmael said. "When he brought Abba to Egypt."

"I suppose so," Hagar said.

That blessing, of course, had been Ishmael. After her mother died, her master sold her. He had grown tired of her and her grief, which had lasted far beyond the proper mourning period. It was unseemly, he'd said. That was how Hagar had ended up serving in Pharaoh's palace.

She'd always been told Pharaoh was a god. Ra incarnate.

The first time she saw him had been from a distance; she'd been kneeling on the river bank, washing his lady's linens, when she saw him sail past in his barge. He'd looked magnificent, with his spear in hand and a lion's pelt draped over his shoulder.

She'd thought to herself, Yes, this is what a living god looks like.

And then Abraham and Sarah came to Egypt, bringing the wrath of their God with them. Pharaoh took Sarah into his home, after Abraham tricked him into believing she was his sister, instead of his wife, and a plague fell upon them all. Hagar remembered lying in bed, feverish and covered in sores, thinking that, of course, it would be a foreign God that would answer her prayer to join her mother in the underworld.

Except Hagar did not die. She was given to Abraham instead, along with other slaves and livestock. A gift from Pharaoh, to appease him and his God. Pharaoh had also suffered from the plague. The last time Hagar saw him, he looked thinner, and he had deep bags under his eyes, his skin having lost its golden luminescence. The blasphemous thought entered Hagar's head that, perhaps, he was only a man after all.

Next to Abraham, with his sunbaked skin and long white beard, it was clear who the gods truly favored.

In Egypt, it wasn't unheard of for slaves to rise to a higher standing. One who pleased her master might become his wife, the new matriarch of his household. Hagar had no such designs on Abraham. Not at first. She was given to Sarah as her personal maid. They did not despise each other then. Actually, Hagar pitied Sarah. She was not only childless, but a foreigner in a strange land, just like Hagar. And at the command of an even stranger God.

Hagar had never met anyone who only worshiped one God before Sarah and Abraham. She found it extremely odd. She'd always known there were people who didn't worship Egypt's gods, down in the Red Lands, where the dead were buried and the demons with the backwards faces dwelt. Hagar used to fear them, but Sarah had shown her only kindness. Until the night she sent her to her husband's tent.

"El has willed that your master be the father of a great nation," Sarah told her. "But not with me. I have grown too old. You, though, you are still young enough to bear children. If you lie with him in my place, perhaps El's will shall be fulfilled through you."

Hagar had not wanted to do it. It may not have been uncommon or unheard of for a master to know his slaves, especially if they were young and beautiful, but Abraham had never shown interest in her before. No one except Sarah. And besides, he was so old.

His tent was dark when Hagar entered, and stank of sweat and camels. Yet Abraham spoke gently to her, and told her, as Sarah had, that she would be the mother of a great nation. Hagar was not naive enough to think she could ever love him, or that he might love her. But she stopped fearing him, as she had in Egypt. It was their love for their son that truly bound them together.

When Ishmael was born, Abraham stood outside the tent, where Hagar squatted on top of the birthing bricks. No one could persuade him to leave, and it was only the midwife's insistence that kept him from running in the moment their son slipped out of her. Ishmael's screams mingled with Hagar's. He looked smaller and more shriveled than she'd imagined, and was covered in blood. But in that moment, as she watched him sob and flail in the midwife's arms, his little hands grasping for warmth from the night air, every other love Hagar had ever felt, even her love for her mother, seemed like a pale imitation of what she now felt for Ishmael.

By the seventh day of travel, Hagar felt less easy with her decision to avoid the cities and roads. Their water skins shrunk in their hands, like dried dates, as the distance between watering holes became greater. That night, they lay shivering and clinging together in the brush. Hagar had not held Ishmael so tightly since he was a child.

It's my fault we've come to this, Hagar thought. I should have made peace with Sarah.

The thought was sudden and unexpected that Hagar almost didn't believe it was hers, but as she listened to her son's teeth chatter, like horse hooves against the earth, while he muttered prayers to El, she knew it was true. Hagar's contempt for her mistress grew with Ishmael, once she felt him in her womb. After all, it was Hagar, not Sarah who the gods had chosen to bless. And someday, it would be her son who would inherit Abraham's wealth. Hagar might also one day displace Sarah in his household, if not his affections. When Sarah looked at her from that point on, Hagar didn't just see envy, but fear as well. If Sarah had been cruel to her, Hagar had been cruel back, in words if not in action.

"Please, El, deliver us from our sufferings…"

Ishmael's voice trembled, and Hagar tightened her grip around him, as if her body could pose a big enough shield against the cold. But gooseflesh covered his skin.

He had wanted to hear the story of how Hagar met El Roi. If she tried to tell him now, her voice would sound as cracked and brittle as her chapped lips.

El Roi was the One who'd seen her when she'd sat alone in the wilderness, who'd comforted her as no one had since her mother's death. He'd affirmed that a great people would, indeed, be born to her. No other god had ever looked upon her, or her suffering, as He had.

The God who saw. She could not have chosen another name for Him.

But He only spoke to her that one time. Sometimes Hagar wondered if she'd imagined Him, sunburnt and exhausted as she'd been. And yet, she still craved his voice as much as the murky waters of spring where He'd come to her. But perhaps this strange God preferred to speak to the likes of Sarah and Abraham over her.

Ishmael groaned. At least, Hagar hoped it was Ishmael. Were the shapes she saw rocks, or animals? Or did the backwards faced demons roam this desert too?

"Have you come to take him away?" she whispered into the dark. "I will not let you take him away from me."

Hagar knew the next night would likely be their last. She tried to remember if there were any springs or wells—any water—nearby, but it was getting almost as hard to think as it was to walk. Before sunset, she and Ishmael had crawled into the bushes that grew along the hills, desperate for the little shade they could offer.

As soon Ishmael fell asleep, Hagar dragged herself away from him. Her arms trembled so much she could barely lift herself, but she couldn't bear to lay next to her son as he died. She collapsed face-down, sending up a cloud of sand that stuck to her face and neck, as if the desert was already preparing to receive her body.

She rolled onto her back. Her head spun so much, she had to clutch the earth to avoid tumbling downhill. She closed her eyes to stop the spinning, and when she opened them again, Hagar was surprised to see it was night.

Ishmael coughed, and Hagar had to turn her face away, grateful she was too parched even to cry, so he wouldn't hear her sobbing. Stars glistened above her, like tear-filled eyes. They cried for her. Ishmael would die first—Hagar was sure of that—but she hoped she would not have to linger long after him, knowing his body was only a few feet away. None of her efforts had been enough to save him. What the animals didn't take from them would eventually be buried by the sand. They would leave no mark of their existence behind. Even Abraham would be quick to forget them, now that he had Isaac.

Perhaps this was all she'd truly been born for: to suffer and be forgotten. Hagar closed her eyes to the stars above. She didn't want to see anymore.

Then she heard the voice.

Hagar gasped and opened her eyes. It was too clear, too powerful to be a hallucination. She had only heard it once before,

but she knew it. She had always known it. It was like a song she'd heard in the womb, and it asked only one thing of her:
"What troubles you, Hagar?"

About the Author

A lifelong resident of Oklahoma, MORGAN WANT received her BA in English from Oklahoma Baptist University, with a minor in professional editing. Her work has been featured in *Heart of Flesh Literary Journal*, *Every Day Fiction*, *Pure in Heart Stories*, and Vine Leaves Press's *50 Give or Take* anthologies. She is currently at work on her first novel.

The Bright Leaf Legacy

Jacqueline Van Hoewyk

SOME PEOPLE SAY TRAGEDIES come in threes. Like the holy trinity, you can't have one without the other two close behind. The Albrights were superstitious folk. And I, being one of them, only had so long to live before I came to realize the power of Providence.

The Father

In the summer of 1964, six months after the surgeon general declared tobacco a threat to public health, my granddaddy Albright fell down dead in the center of his tobacco field. When your granddaddy is struck by lightning in the center of his livelihood while you, nine years old, can only watch, high trees swaying like willing and better targets all around, you tell me what you believe—that was one.

Grannie Winnifred knew it too. When Granddaddy dropped, she didn't skip a beat. Poured her too-sour lemonade, passed it around to me and the rest of the farmhands waiting out the storm on the porch, and began to sing, "I'll answer, dear Lord, with my hand in thine, I'll go where you want me to go," knowing she was next. The farm was hers now.

The Son

It took three years before fate struck again. In the meantime, Grannie Winnie lulled us into believing she could keep the farm running indefinitely through sheer force of will. After Granddaddy was buried and the tobacco sent off to auction that first year, Mama took to hiding in the curing barn just to get away from Daddy's frenetic energy. It was as if all the electricity that had struck our land had spread like roots and erupted up into Grannie and Daddy. They worked twice as hard to placate the farmhands who were afraid of being replaced by tractors or reduced need, due to the new loosened regulations the government hoped would spur the market. Everything in service of keeping the bright leaf going. After the declaration, the government, of course, had its backup plans. We, however, did not.

As for Mama, despite her protestations that this wasn't the life she'd signed up for, the raised voices I heard from my bed at night, Grannie made her put all that time hiding away to use. The barn became her makeshift studio—sewing dresses for the women of The Borough. Her way to foster goodwill with the community. Problem was, the cracks were already there, and no amount of skill with the bright leaf or a needle and thread could stitch our family back together.

Good Friday, 1967. Seedlings ready for planting, and me up in the balcony at church, lying beneath a pew, licking chocolate off my fingers from stolen eggs we weren't supposed to open 'til Sunday. That's when I heard it. A whooshing sound. Like a curtain hastily dropped on a stage full of naked actors not ready to play their parts. Then the thunk and smack of wood on wood. I bolted upright.

She lay near the pulpit, floral cotton dress rolled above her stockinged feet, round arms splayed wide, a vision of Christ himself on the cross—Grannie Winnie. Only her cross was the ladder she'd been balancing on, trying to hang the Easter decorations while everyone else had supper downstairs. Had they heard? Would they recognize true need when there was food laid out in front of them?

I flew down the stairs two and three at a time. When I reached her, I tried to pull the ladder from her still form, but someone lifted me from behind, strong arms beneath my armpits. I kicked and twisted, but no use.

"Ambulance is on its way."

"Daddy!" He didn't let go of me, even when I stopped squirming, his knuckles white with strain, clasped over my clay stained overalls. Then I saw his eyes.

He knew. The day our lord died, and Grannie Winnie called home—that was two.

By the time we got to the hospital, we knew Grannie was gone, but that didn't stop Mama. She rushed through the doors to where we sat in the waiting room, waving Grannie's floral carpet bag she'd brought from home. She scanned the room as if looking for signs of the one person who held us all together.

"I should've been there." Her voice rose and fell in pitch as if someone had tweaked her like a radio dial mid-sentence, and my heart pounded in my ears because Mama always said she wouldn't be caught dead in church.

Daddy didn't respond, just pulled her into a hug and smoothed her fraying auburn braid.

I'd risen to greet her as well, but seeing them entwined like this, I hesitated. They'd been together long before me, known Grannie longer. They deserved a moment alone. I stood back, watching them comfort each other.

"It was inevitable," Daddy whispered into Mama's hair.

"What does that even mean?" Freeing herself from his grip, Mama tugged at her braid, making it wild again. She fixed her eyes on me as if this were all my fault, as if she'd known I'd been hiding away on my own instead of helping Grannie with the decorations. I picked dirt from my nails rather than argue the finer points of the Albright superstition to the self-proclaimed Californian who'd saddled herself to Daddy on his way home from Korea.

"How'd you get here, anyway?" Daddy asked, snatching Grannie Winnie's bag from Mama and dropping it onto an empty chair. All semblance of tenderness between them vanished, and they were back at it. I realize now, maybe that's why I'd held back. Avoiding the inevitable burst as two forces of nature came too close, had no choice but to repel each other.

"Reggie brought me."

"That boy's got enough to be getting on with at the farm. He don't need to be seen escorting white women around."

"How else was I supposed to get here?" Mama had never gotten her license, seeing it as one more manacle of obligation that would tie her to errands for the rest of her life. Though she knew how to drive, she preferred to flit around on foot and take rides as they came.

A doctor appeared at the end of the hallway, his eyes scanning the room, which was a useless gesture as we were the only people apart from the staff there. Seeming to brace himself, he approached with an efficient stride and extended a hand. He was the one who'd rolled Grannie in back when we'd gotten here.

Mama stepped between them, knocking Daddy's hand out the way. "Why don't you just spit it out, doctor—she's dead. Isn't that right?"

I held my breath. No one could cut to the chase like Mama.

"Mr. Albright is already aware, Ma'am." He nodded toward Daddy, and perfunctorily added, "We did what we could."

Daddy nodded slowly, handed the doctor Grannie's frayed carpet bag, which had really only seen one true vacation to the Outer Banks in its lifetime, turned on his heel, and walked out the door.

Mama's eyes bulged like two sacks of marbles fixing to erupt in a torrent of jangled aquamarine glass.

The doctor, to his credit, attempted to maintain a sympathetic smile while assuring her Daddy had taken care of everything, that Mrs. Albright would be ready for her last goodbyes whenever they set a date for the funeral. His smile faltered when she spat in his face.

And that's when I knew something in Mama had broken. An acidic taste like Grannie's lemonade rose in my throat, and I wanted to flee, find Daddy, pull him back inside, make him hold on to Mama until she agreed they were in this together, until she promised to stop locking the barn door when he was home, until she promised she'd do everything to make sure the farm would survive because it was up to them now. God had willed it, after all. Instead, I swallowed the memory of lemonade I'd never partake of again and waited for Mama to tell me what to do next.

She insisted on driving us home. In one fluid motion, she waved Reggie into the passenger seat and took the wheel while I climbed into the back of the station wagon. Mama didn't speak, only muttered to herself while Reggie and I traded wary glances. Four years older than me, Reggie had been around since he was old enough to sucker tobacco, long enough to know Mama, and this was strange even for her. She continued like this for twenty minutes, speeding past stop signs, veering into traffic, never pausing for a response and barely stopping for breath.

"He shouldn't have to do this. Damnit, Winnifred. It's not fair. We always wanted… Joel wanted…He Promised…One day—"

I cut in, my nerves frayed from the drive, unable to take it anymore. "But Daddy said—"

Mama silenced me with a wave of her hand. "Your daddy don't know his heart from a hole in the ground."

Reggie, agreeable as he was (so agreeable I knew he'd been the one to suggest waiting outside so as not to make a scene by entering the white hospital, whereas Mama would've relished it) tried to smooth things over. "I reckon he just gone home. Those seedlings is needy."

"Right." Mama nodded, breathless, all the wind gone out of her. They'd be talking about her spitting into Dr. Beachum's face for years. "He'll need another set of hands for transplanting now, won't he?"

"I can do it," I said.

"You've got school."

"Reggie don't go," I responded automatically, falling into our old argument. I hated school and didn't see the point since I'd be taking over the farm one day anyway.

"Reggie wishes he could, now don't you?"

"Suppose I do, if I'm honest. But I don't want to be anywhere I'm not wanted, neither."

"Now, if that isn't the most goddamned honest thing I ever heard. And amen!"

"Mama!"

"Don't Mama me. You don't know the half of it, girl. Stuck up in your trees. Playing with those damn dogs. Oblivious to the world around you. When someone isn't wanted, it tears a hole inside. You either hide who you are and try to blend in, or you fight. Either way, you're killing yourself."

I clenched my eyes to stem the tears threatening to erupt. I imagined Grannie Winnie scolding Mama, assuring her God has a plan for everyone. How could she not see what had been laid out for her? It was her turn now. Hers and Daddy's.

"Miss Sage…you missed the turn," Reggie said. "Miss Sage?" He craned his neck, but the road disappeared behind us into the dark.

"Well now, I guess that means we're heading to town."

Mama parked in front of RJ's soda shop. When it was clear we weren't going home, Reggie and I followed her inside. The three of us slipped into a corner booth near the windows facing the train tracks. Mama ordered malted milkshakes and a plate of fries to share.

I stared at my reflection in the dark glass, wondering what Daddy was really doing right now. I hoped Boots and Scout were at least keeping him company. My two hound dogs always cheered me up. The sound of Mama's laughter, high and false, pulled my attention.

She'd climbed into the booth opposite me to sit with Reggie. Her hair was a mess, frayed strands of her braid sticking out at odd angles, and she had her arms wrapped around him, cradling his head to her chest as if this sixteen-year-old boy were her baby. She rocked him side to side, tears streaming down her face, laughing all the while. I don't think I'd ever seen Mama cry before that day and it froze my guts. Without Grannie here to tell her to mind herself, Mama seemed to be searching for trouble, figuring on a tongue lashing that would never come again.

"What are we going to do now?" She petted Reggie's head and shushed him while he sat rigid, trying to avoid my gaze.

A group of men at the counter turned and narrowed their eyes at us. It was challenge enough for Mama to have brought Reggie into the diner, but the way she was carrying on laid a spotlight over our table. After a moment, perhaps weighing hunger against righteous indignation, the men shook their heads and turned back to their food.

"Mama, I want to go home." The milkshake was sickly sweet, the fries were soggy, and Mama's behavior had only become more concerning since we'd left the hospital. We just needed to get home and find Daddy, and things would be okay.

"Reggie isn't finished with his shake.".

I gave Reggie a pleading look, and he nodded. He might be agreeable, but he was my friend, not Mama's pet. We'd spent our lives roaming the woods together with Boots and Scout while our parents worked the field.

"I'm really not that hungry, and Mr. Joel might need me back—"

"He doesn't need anything, and you aren't your father, Reginald. Now take it easy once in a while and drink your shake. Life isn't all about work."

At the mention of his father, Reggie fell silent. Mr. Forester had been killed the previous year while walking home from a neighboring farm. Hit and run. Most people in town believed it hadn't been an accident.

I tried to meet his gaze, to tell him with my eyes I was sorry. Mama was clearly not herself; she'd become untethered without Grannie to smooth her out. Reggie didn't look up. He was too busy guzzling down the rest of his shake.

Clearly believing Reggie to be on her side, Mama turned her attention to the men at the counter. "And what are you do-gooders looking at?" She drawled as if her milkshake was spiked.

Addressed directly, the group at the counter no longer saw

it necessary to shoot covert glances between bites of their egg salad sandwiches. They spun on their stools. One of them jabbed at us with his sandwich as he spoke.

"Ma'am, this ain't the place or the time to start trouble." His jowled cheeks shook as he spoke.

"Never said it was, sir. If you can't tell, this family is having a bit of a hard time today. Now, I'd appreciate it if you mind your own business and stop giving us that stink eye." She smiled sweetly. "Please."

"Brightleaf county is my business, Ma'am." He tapped his sandwich on the black leather-bound book resting next to his chipped white plate on the counter. And now I recognized him. Strange how when you see someone outside their context, it's hard to know who they are. He was Reverend Buncombe, from the neighboring town of Pinesboro, who'd given the sermon last week while our usual pastor was ill. Of course, Mama wouldn't know that, seeing as she never came to church with us.

Reggie stood. "I'm finished, Miss Sage. My ma will be wondering where I am."

Mama, without turning from the men at the counter, put her hand on Reggie's shoulder and pushed him back into the booth. "No, she won't. She'll be glad you got dinner someplace else tonight. She can put her feet up and relax, not having to cook for you for once."

I stood without thinking and stepped between Mama and the reverend. In the sweetest voice I could muster, I said, "I very much enjoyed your sermon the other day. My daddy, Joel Albright, may be calling on you for some help tomorrow, if you'd oblige. You see, my grannie, she…" And lord help me if I wasn't able to conjure up some tears. A right miracle, as I felt more like vomiting on his shoes by that point.

The reverend licked the grease from his lips with a flick of his pale tongue and rubbed his palms together. A scattering of crumbs fell to the floor between us. Then he placed his hands on my shoulders and leaned into my face as if to see better. His breath smelled of sour mayonnaise and chewing tobacco.

"Why, if it isn't young Prudence! Of course I knew your grannie well, a fine woman. Managed so well after Al's passing. So, this must be...Miss Sage?" He held out a smooth palm to Mama. "Why, you made the dress for Bettie's cotillion! The only reason that girl got a husband, I swear! Not to my sweet girl's face, of course. But dear lord, he does work in mysterious ways. Come over here, Miss Sage. Let me thank you for my grandchildren."

Mama chuckled and stood, straightening her skirt. Her smile was wide and wicked and my heart froze, fearing another incident like at the hospital.

"Now Miss Sage, I do appreciate your trade, but we'd also like to welcome you in worship." His hand hung in the air, expectant.

"Like you'd welcome my son-in-law here?" Sage cupped Reggie's cheek with her palm. Reggie looked pained, but at this point wasn't going to argue.

My mouth flopped open, but I gathered my wits before the reverend had a chance to collect his and clasped his hand between mine. It was fleshy and pink like a pig's rump, but I squeezed it tight, assured him Grannie's death had been very hard on Mama, it being so fresh and all, and that her jokes weren't often the most savory when she was grieving. Then I added, without glancing back, that Mama would be happy to make dresses for his grandchildren in the future, for free.

Something must've clicked in Mama's mind too, for she glanced at Reggie and her face fell. She let me have the last word. Then the three of us hurried out of the soda shop. This time she allowed Reggie to take the wheel without complaint, but once we hit the winding country roads, he had to pull over to vomit up his milkshake. I offered to drive, but they waved me off, leaving me to stew in the back on what the big fuss about coming to town was if we were going to get in trouble every time we ventured off the farm. For Mama, encountering the other members of The Borough was like some sort of anthropological research expedition, always having to poke and prod to get an expected reaction, surprised when they said or did something new, because, like it or not, times were changing, though never fast enough for her taste.

When Reggie parked in front of the house, Boots and Scout bayed and scrabbled at the running board until I threw them the french fries I'd pocketed. Reggie waved goodnight and headed off toward the treeline where his family's cottage sat nestled in the woods. He was comfortable navigating the forest at night, whereas I was always worried about the ghost in the woods. The hounds loped after him until they reached Daddy's campfire, a faint glow beside the dark of the forest. He had set up camp for the night beside the seedbeds. Frosts were still common this time of year and he'd need to cover the seedlings with canvas and wake early to inspect for bugs.

Mama retreated to her barn under pretense of finishing the flock of Easter dresses she'd have to deliver alone without Winnifred to quell any disapproval from parents at her flagrant disregard for a young woman's modesty. Mama's costume designer roots and west coast origins were always a selling point to the girls, who never informed their parents of the exact cut or hemline of what they'd commissioned with their daddy's money. And it had been Winnifred's task to smooth out the ruffled feathers, citing Mama's ignorance as an outsider while touting her credentials with such grace that it left husbands, wives, and daughters mutually happy with their purchase.

I was left with nothing to do but to go into the empty house and go to bed. I stared up at the moonlight-dappled ceiling and asked God how Granny Winnie would feel at the sight of the three of us, each in our own world on the very night of her death, and then I cried, wishing for one more of her biscuits slathered in jam, for one more hug to inhale the scent of thyme and bright leaf that hung on her apron like perfume, but all I had left was the tartness of her lemonade brewing in my chest, and it burned. Maybe God hadn't gifted our family with his blessing. Was it possible this Godstruck land had been cursed?

The Holy Spirit

I saw many things from my tree. The organized movements of Daddy and the farmhands at harvest time, tiny specks among the man-high rows of yellowing tobacco. The church ladies, with their wide-brimmed hats and white gloves, who, despite their public disapproval, still visited Mama to have dresses made for special occasions. And now, with the harvest over and the tobacco off to Durham, the flocks of geese had begun to fly overhead daily, trumpeting a proud declaration of their journey south. Even Reggie, who'd helped as much as he could between going off to school and taking care of his mama, who'd taken ill that summer, flitted in wide spirals, avoiding Mama since the day Grannie had died. Everyone came and went, so sure of their purpose, while I just watched, waiting for number three.

Fall 1967. The first day of deer season. Our neighbor, the veterinarian Mr. Melvin, took Daddy hunting. The house was empty again. Only the echo of those summer voices and the nutty perfume of toasted leaves to remind me how the bright leaf had held us together. But even geese come back, so I figured it was just the season. With Daddy out of the house, Mama had also stolen away, locking herself in the barn again to sew. Only when I got there, put my ear to the wooden door, I couldn't hear her sewing machine nor smell her smoking as she worked—the one bad habit she'd picked up in this place, she always said. The one good one being how to fire a gun. And off my mind went, whirring to see Mama, rifle raised, taking a ten-point buck while Daddy and Mr. Melvin watched in awe. That was Mama, always a surprise, though she'd borne her new role as Grannie Winnie's replacement well, getting us through the harvest with healthy servings of dry cornbread and her unsweet tea, which left something to be desired, but still gave me hope.

The rough wood against my ear brought me back to my senses, and I reminded myself I was nearly thirteen and it wasn't so grown up to be dreaming all the time.

Grannie Winnie always said to Mama, "Problem with having only one child, no one to play with but themselves. Lost in the clouds and not a lick of sense for reality." But she'd been an only child herself, so I knew she meant well. Besides, she'd sing me to sleep with songs of the magic of the farm and the ghost in the woods who protected our field. Mama, on the other hand, would purse her lips and tug on her braid anytime Grannie spoke of nature's magic or God's will. But she was an only child too, as was Daddy, so I knew, deep down they understood. And that's why the three of us were destined to be alone, even in each other's company. Strange things a child will tell themselves to stave off loneliness, but that was what I believed then.

Since Mama wasn't in the house or the barn, I went to my tree for a better view and to wait for Daddy's return. My tree was evidence of the magic of this land. Dogwoods usually never grew so large, but mine was perfect for climbing and for spying, as I mentioned. It stood sentinel along the edge of the field at the entrance to the woods.

I climbed with the practiced motion of a girl who spent her days running barefoot through these woods and leaned into the familiar crook of my favorite branch. Boots and Scout waited at the base of the tree, tongues lolling, until they grew bored and flew off into the woods at the slightest noise, leaving a cloud of pine needles in their wake. The sun was setting, and Daddy, gone since before sunrise, had to be on his way back. I trusted my hounds to sniff him out and turned to the house to watch for Mama.

As if in response to my thoughts, a light flicked on in their bedroom upstairs. Her silhouette moved across the window. Maybe she'd been out delivering a garment and was changing for dinner. The light went out. Sunlight faded around me and a cool breeze tickled my cheek. Daddy didn't like me climbing in the dark, but it was their fault they weren't here, so I waited.

A few moments later, the slam of the screen door. Expecting to hear Mama call me to dinner, I slid forward on the branch, stretching my legs to climb down. Instead, I heard the ignition of a car roar to life and saw the flash of headlights against the side of the house.

Before I could ponder what was happening, a peal of laughter rippled through the woods behind me—Daddy. And the sound was so shocking, I flinched as if slapped. I hadn't heard him laugh since before Granddaddy died.

I whirled back toward the house to see if Mama had heard, had felt that note of lightness, the promise of the future. All I saw was the station wagon bumping down the gravel road away from the farm, and a sudden flood of energy coursed through me. Again, the three of us were dewdrops on spider's silk, sliding away from each other. Intent on catching at least one of them, I scrabbled down my branch, and, while reaching for the next, tumbled into open air.

The farmhouse loomed before me like the moon, inverted and all wrong. Soft, slippery tongues lapped at my fingers and I raised my head. I was dangling over Daddy's shoulder, my hair brushing his legs. A tang of iron and urine hung in the air. Beside Daddy walked Mr. Melvin, his own prize slung over his shoulder.

"Keep still," Daddy grunted. "Your arm's broken."

I blinked, tried to fling myself upright, but my head spun and I folded into his grip.

He laid me in bed.

"Where's Mama?"

He didn't answer, just pulled my quilt up to my chin and left the room.

When I woke, colors swirled to form the hexagonal pieces of the quilt Grannie Winnie had made me when I was born. Atop it sat a roll of white gauze. Mr. Melvin leaned over me and gathered up his tools.

"Don't climb any trees for a while, eh?"

I winced. Through my window, the deer hung from the oak that shaded our house, waiting to be skinned.

Mr. Melvin left my room and met Daddy beyond the door. I saw him pat Daddy on the shoulder and guide him toward the door, whispering. As they were standing in the entryway on the other side of my wall, I heard them easily enough.

"I'm sorry Joel," Mr. Melvin said. "I'm sure she'll come back."

And that was three.

The deer hung for two weeks. And I learned there's worse things than death. There's the smell and the flies. There's the blank stare gone milky as you're ripped to shreds by nature, a blank stare Daddy's own eyes echoed as he rocked on the porch facing the gravel road, day after day while the field withered. Then there's responsibility. Those who take it, and those who run. I cut down the deer. There's those who believe and those who don't. Grunting, one arm still pinned to my chest, I managed the wheelbarrow, dumped the thing into the woods for the turkey vultures to finish off. Then I turned back to my farm because I am an Albright, I am one of the believers, and it was my turn.

About the Author

Born in Japan and raised in the swampy Lowcountry of South Carolina, JACQUELINE VAN HOEWYK'S writing focuses on outsiders seeking their place in the world, family, and how place shapes us. She loves history, mystery, and magic found in the everyday, which she writes about on her Substack, Collecting Dust. The Bright Leaf Legacy offers a first look at the family at the center of her first novel. Jacqueline lives with her husband and two children in North Carolina.

Diary of an Empire

Shay Galloway

December, 1908
Goshen County, Wyoming

ARRIVED IN TORRINGTON Thanksgiving Day. Thankfully the weather held out on the train and we managed not to freeze in that drafty carriage. Baby Howard was an angel all the way over. Of course, he's still plenty small and spending all his time sleeping when he's not eating. Even when he's eating too, I suppose. I kept him tucked in my coat, nice and warm. Chaz met us at the station, and took us right out to the plot. It was night by the time we arrived. I could hardly even make out the shape of the house. It's just small. Sod like the one I was born and raised, just one room right now, as it's just the three of us. But Chaz promised me my clapboard house soon.

    He and the others have called this place Empire. It will be our Empire, he says. Someday we'll have a general store and churches and a school. It will be a Western outpost for Colored folk.

    I must admit it can be difficult to see what he envisions. I look out and all I see is dust and scrub. The winter wind bites cold. How Chaz plans to farm with no water, I cannot even begin to guess.

March, 1909

    I have gotten so lonely and bleak some days it's all I can do to not go out and scream into the bitter wind. Since the weather has started warming up and the ground thawing, Chaz has spent so much of the time out considering the fields or off in Torrington ordering this or that. There are the other men's wives, of course, but I feel so small and out of place compared to them. They are all at least a decade older than me and seasoned mothers with many children. Though I appreciate the space Chaz and I get to spend alone (finally), I sometimes envy the others' full houses. Like Otis and Sarah Taylor, who have not only their own kids, but their brother and his child. I miss my own sisters.

Baby Howard is growing fat and fine, but his teeth are coming in and all day and night he's crying, gnawing angrily on his little fists. One day he was carrying on so, I cried too, pacing back and forth on the packed dirt floor, bouncing him with no relief, when a knock came at the door. I at first did not want to answer it, but I was so desperate for some reprieve, I did, despite Howard's wailing and my own haggard appearance. It was one of the Taylor brothers—Baseman or Bozeman—something of the like. They're somewhat related to Chaz, cousins or by marriage I haven't quite worked out yet. He's a big man, I've seen him out in the fields. Chaz told me he was widowed just last year, left his little girl Elsie about four years old. I'll admit his size initially frightened me, but he knocked on the door that day just to check on me and the baby after hearing Howard carrying on. He took Howard out in the sunshine for a short while and let me have a moment's peace.

June, 1909

At last the warm days outnumber the cold, the crops are in the dust, and things are getting on. I went with the other wives into Torrington to do our own goods stock. Baseman joined us since the other men were busy in the fields (if you can even call them that, given it is mostly just dust and rocks.) Baseman says he wasn't meant to be a farmer, but it's all he knows, so he'll gladly escort us into town if ever we need, give him an excuse to stop scratching in the dirt for a minute.

There isn't much to Torrington. Even less than there was in Westerville, we have no choice but to shop where everyone else shops. It was alright I suppose. We had eyes on us the whole time, especially on Baseman, but no one stopped us. We didn't try to haggle, we didn't mingle. We made our purchases and hurried home.

September, 1909

We have a schoolhouse! I thought maybe I could step in and teach, be a teacher just like Mama had hoped I would, but another Taylor brother is set to join us here in Empire to run it. Reverend Russell. Rev, as Chaz and the others call him. Chaz says he'll likely need a hand with all these kids though, and probably wouldn't be opposed to my assistance.

Little Howard is up and walking now. I can barely keep up, for even with his little legs, he is fast.

February, 1910

Chaz's mother has arrived. We added a little room for her at the back of the house. She's grieving in her widowhood, but she and Howard love each other so. Her presence makes me miss my own mother all the more. Perhaps soon we will visit.

September, 1910

Our little Lena was born last month. Howard is in love. She looks just like my sister Annie—who I hope is doing well, her little one must be causing all sorts of mischief these days.

October, 1911

Crops all failed. Again.
I am pregnant. Again. I no longer have the energy to help at the school.

April, 1912

Baseman hung up his plow and left Otis and Sarah's house for good. He has, of late, become sullen and short. He is certain we are all being sabotaged, him especially. He stays in Torrington through the week and comes back to Empire each Sunday to visit Elsie, who will remain under Sarah's care. We also, as of this month, have a post office. It's hardly more than a desk in Otis' house, but it is official.

May, 1912

A man came to the door. A white man with a mustache so like my father's I nearly thought it was him when I first opened the door. But my father would never look at me or any like woman with such condescension. He didn't even say hello, just "My pig is missing." I told him I hadn't seen it, but I'd keep watch and lead it back his way should I find it. Then he inquired after my husband "If I had one." And when I told him Chaz was out in the field, he demanded to look around the plot for his pig. I told him there's no pig here, we don't even have any outbuildings. He could look for himself. Then I shut the door without another word. Mama Susan and I sat against the door, keeping the kids in until the man went away. He made his way to Sarah and Lizzie's houses until Lizzie's oldest boy stepped up and assured the man the pig was not here and he best go back to his own home and look again.

August, 1912

The crops are fat and green. Every single one of them. Finally.

We have another daughter; Ava.

November, 1912

These white men need to better maintain their livestock.

May, 1913

Crops are in the ground and seem to be taking. Howard has been doing well learning his numbers and letters. Some man was in Torrington yesterday preaching that we Negroes ought to only be welcome to shop in town at night and tried handing

Mr. Allred of the general store a flyer reading "No Indians, No Negroes, No Mexicans," admonishing him to hang it up in his front window, passed it over right in front of us without making eye contact with anyone other than Mr. Allred. "I'll consider it," Mr. Allred said, and the man went on to the next shop. Allred set the flyer down on the counter and accepted our transactions without making a comment on it. I am hoping money is money to him, regardless of whose hands it comes from. If Torrington starts to deny us, where else do we have to go? It's a full day's ride at *least* anywhere else.

June, 1913

It appears most of the Torrington shopkeepers have paid no mind to that horrid man. We didn't spot more than two of those flyers in town.

August, 1913

Baseman has been spending more days in Empire lately, and is now given to fits where it seems he's been taken over by another man entirely. One who is angry, and has no sense of who we are or where he is. Sarah and Otis tried to talk him into seeking treatment during one of his lucid moments, but he ran back off to Torrington and carries on as if all is well, returning each Sunday as usual.

October, 1913

We are to have another child.

November 4, 1913

Baseman failed to show on Sunday, with no word. He has never failed to show. The men all went to town after supper to inquire of him. A dread has fallen over Empire while we wait for their return, hoping against hope it's nothing more than illness that has him bedridden. But we all heard about the man in the state penitentiary last year—that poor man of our own kind who never got the chance to live out his sentence.

The Blood of Englishmen

The men have returned. Baseman has been taken by the sheriff. It seems he had an episode that caused some disturbance in town. By all accounts, he caused no one harm, and did not fight when the deputies took him. When Rev asked on what charges our Baseman is being held, the sheriff simply said, "For being crazy." Since Torrington has no jailhouse, he is being kept at the hotel, where all guests and all of Torrington can see him on display. The men have telegraphed lawyers in Cheyenne.

November 7, 1913

After three days, Baseman has been released from his imprisonment, both from the sheriff's deputies and this earthly realm. It sickens me to have to write such words. Since we have the fewest and smallest children and so the easiest to move, Otis brought him to our house, laid him on the table like an offering of penance. The papers say he died of "medical conditions" but the battering of his poor gentle body says otherwise. How alone and frightened he must have been, with no familiar faces to call him back from the dark wilds of his wandering mind—only fists and chokeholds and burning cigar ends. His last moments just a carnival curiosity for soulless townsfolk.

"Equality" State, they call this place. But they're just like everywhere else. They'll tell you it's a Southern thing; that kind of thing just doesn't happen out West. They wear the stamp of Wild West, build up this place as one where people are free to do as they please, be as they please, without the constraints of society like the East, like the South. No, they'll say, those kinds of things just don't happen *here*. But this place was settled by men of the South and the East.

What do we tell the children? This is what happens when you step out of line—that is what the white men would want us to tell them. But the only line Baseman crossed was his own mind. Instead we'll have to tell the children that this is what happens to us, no matter where we go, this happens. They'll tell you all you've got to do is mind your own business, stay in your place. But they'll also be minding your business, crowding into your space.

There is talk among the men about seeking justice, but from whom? It was the law that did this.

What is to become of Elsie?

January, 1914

I cannot bear another winter here. I know Spring will come, and with it, the warmth of the sun. But that is all. The sun will grow too hot, the land too arid and dry, all the hopeful sprouts will only wither.

I know Nebraska was hardly an improvement on the weather, but at least there, we'd have the strength of community. *Real* community, not a ragged handful of families. We are hardly more than a brittle skeleton exposed to the mercy of desperate vultures.

March, 1914

Another girl.

August, 1914

Crops are gone. And I am done.

September, 1914

Chaz has relented. He will leave next week to follow a lead on a new homestead.

November, 1915
Dewitty, Nebraska

At last, I have a clapboard house complete with wooden floors.

My mother is at the door.

Historical note: Empire was a small African American community on the Wyoming-Nebraska border established in 1908 by various members of the Speese family. At 17 with a new baby, Hannah Rachel Rosetta "Rose" Meehan Speese arrived as the youngest and newest of the wives who settled the arid homestead. After several years of failed farming and racial tension—including the killing of

Baseman Taylor—most residents left by the 1920s. Today, all that remains of Empire are two historical markers and a few dilapidated structures. Rose and Charles were among the first of the families to relocate, first to Nebraska and then to South Dakota and Minnesota. Rose eventually bore seventeen children, all but two of whom survived to adulthood.

About the Author

SHAY GALLOWAY studied creative writing at Utah State University and received an MFA from Roosevelt University, Chicago. Her work has been featured in several journals and mags. Her debut novel, *The Valley of Sage and Juniper* was released March 2023 with Running Wild/RIZE Press. She currently teaches college English and resides in Washington with her husband and sons.

Acknowledgments

Publishing an anthology is a tremendous exercise in collaboration and cooperation. It takes dozens of people working together to write, select, edit, design, and publish the stories you've read here. I am incredibly grateful for each and every contribution that made this anthology possible.

Thank you first and foremost to every single writer who submitted to our contest. We received 110 submissions! Each writer put both their trust and their heart on the line. We acknowledge the vulnerability of the submission process, and we thank you for allowing us to consider your story. Whether your work was selected or not, we recognize the effort and dedication it takes to write, and we wish you continued success on your writing journey—whether with us or elsewhere.

Thank you to all of our volunteer judges. I could not possibly read every submission myself. Even if I could, my perspective alone would not be sufficient to fairly evaluate each story. It takes a team of intelligent, thoughtful, and well-meaning individuals to read, evaluate, and provide constructive feedback on each story, making the selection process possible. Thank you, judges, for giving your time and energy to support us, these writers, and the art of storytelling in general.

Thank you to our cover designer, Steph Ross, for creating a beautiful cover that reflects both the history and the compelling narratives found within this anthology. Thank you to Inanna Arthen, our interior layout designer, who handles her work with professionalism and efficiency every time. Thank you to my interns, Evelyn Nygren and Henna Schecter, for assisting me throughout the entire short story contest—from story selection to editing, design, and publication.

And finally, thank you to you, dear reader. I cannot thank you enough. We don't do this work for ourselves—though we love it—we do it for you. Without readers, there is little reason to do the work at all. Thank you for reading, for supporting us and these talented authors and creators, and for valuing history and storytelling. Please carry forward some of the lessons from these stories and share them with others. Thank you!

About History Through Fiction

Founded in 2019 by Minnesota author and historian Colin Mustful, History Through Fiction is an independent press dedicated to publishing high-quality historical fiction. We believe that strong storytelling is strengthened by historical integrity. The novels we publish are grounded in careful research and reflect a deep respect for the historical process, offering readers narratives that are both engaging and authentic.

At History Through Fiction, we strive to bring history to life through compelling stories that connect readers to the people, places, and events of the past while highlighting their continued relevance today.

If you enjoyed this anthology, please consider leaving a review. It's the best way to support us and our authors. Plus, you'll be helping other readers discover this great story.

Learn more at www.historythroughfiction.com

www.ingramcontent.com/pod-product-compliance
Lightning Source LLC
LaVergne TN
LVHW040105080526
838202LV00045B/3782